THE QUAN SHANG OPERA

IN THE HOUSE OF DELIRIOUS HARMONY

Erich von Neff

THE QUAN SHANG OPERA

IN THE HOUSE OF DELIRIOUS HARMONY

Histria Romance

Las Vegas ◊ Chicago ◊ Palm Beach

Published in the United States of America by
Histria Books
7181 N. Hualapai Way, Ste. 130-86
Las Vegas, NV 89166 USA
HistriaBooks.com

Histria Romance is an imprint of Histria Books dedicated to the finest Romance books from leading authors around the world. Titles published under the imprints of Histria Books are distributed worldwide.

This is a work of fiction. Names, characters, places, and incidents are either the product of the author's imagination or are used fictitiously. Any resemblance to actual persons, living or dead, is entirely coincidental.

Library of Congress Control Number: 2024944045

ISBN 978-1-59211-505-1 (softbound)
ISBN 978-1-59211-522-8 (eBook)

1

Geary Quan looked through the faded curtains out to the empty street. He glanced at his watch. The plane had landed at the San Francisco International Airport two hours ago, and still she hadn't arrived. A pickup truck drove up to the warehouse across the street. Geary Quan saw two men get out. One of them opened the door of the warehouse. Geary thought of phoning the police, but here in Chinatown where there were gangs and drug deals it was best to keep his mouth shut. Shortly, the two men reappeared carrying a crate. He could hear one of them swearing at the other as they put the crate in the bed of the pickup, then they flipped up the tailgate, climbed in the cab of the pickup, and drove off.

The street was empty again. Geary wished that someone else would drive by or that a drunk would pass, anything to fill the time. Where was she? Problems with Customs maybe. Just then he saw a yellow cab round the corner. The cab driver jammed on the brakes, then slammed the door. A man in a turban walked briskly forward and banged on Geary's door. Geary opened it hesitantly. The cab driver held out his hand. "Thirty dollars, please," he said politely, but firmly.

"Thirty dollars?"

"That's what I said."

"Wait then."

Geary walked into the apartment. He opened his dresser drawer. There were coins and bills of various denominations scattered in the drawer. He grabbed a ten, a five, another five, and some ones. Weren't there larger denominations? The ten, the fives, eight dollars in ones and the rest in change would have to do.

Geary rushed to the door, afraid the cab driver wouldn't wait. The cabbie extended his hand.

"Both hands," Geary said. Geary put the currency and the coins into the cabbie's outstretched hands. The cabbie opened the front door of the cab and spread the money out on the front seat. He extended his hand again slowly but forcefully. "I am not going to give you a tip," Geary said. The cabbie swore in a language that Geary did not understand, then switched to English. "Chinese are all the same," he shouted. The cabbie now rapped on the rear window. Geary heard a door open and close on the other side, then the cab drove off.

At first, he could only see an outline of her, as if she were a dark shadow just across from him. She remained motionless looking down and not at him. Slowly she walked forward.

"I am Geary Quan," he said quietly. She walked past him, stepped onto the sidewalk and

stood in front of the door, waiting. Geary wished that she was a white girl, a Mexican girl, or a Black girl or that she had gotten out of the cab drinking and smoking a cigarette. She seemed so aloof and so traditional. Geary shrugged his shoulders. He may as well let his future wife in the door.

2

Guangzhou, the capital of Guangdong Province in the People's Republic of China.
Mei Fang

Chung laid a piece of red paper flat on the table. She picked up two eggs which the hens had laid yesterday, which had just been boiled. Mei Fang cracked them open by snapping them against the wooden table. Quickly she pulled off the shells and laid one of the eggs on the red paper. Mei Fang rolled the egg back and forth on the paper, and then the ends, until the egg was just as red as the color of the paper. Then she rolled the other egg on the paper. The red eggs were now put on a plate with the outline of a blue fish. Several spoonfuls of rice were heaped next to them. Mei Fang now lit a small candle which she held in her hand.

"San San, come here," her mother said softly. San San stepped quietly into the room. She smiled, restraining herself. Red is considered a lucky color in China. On her past birthdays San San had received one red egg with rice. Today she was receiving two red eggs with rice. Was something good going to happen? San San blew gently on the candle until the flame flickered out. Mei Fang watched as her daughter ate her rice with chopsticks. How delicate her hands were and what smooth gracious movements she had, even while eating.

San San smiled at her mother, then took a small bite out of one of the eggs. She paused, savoring the egg, then continued eating in the same slow deliberate fashion. Her father entered the room. San San put down the egg. "What is this, Confucian times," he said laughing. "This is your birthday, eat." San San continued eating the egg, feeling quite guilty as she did so. "You needn't worry about me," her father said, patting his belly, which was really more due to a slouch than to a middle-age spread. Bao Wei Chung smiled. He was very proud of his daughter. Only two months ago she had graduated from Sun Yat-Sen University with a degree in economics and here she was just twenty years old. She had always been first or nearly first in any class she had taken. When a subject was difficult for her, she had studied far into the night. At times, he had been concerned about her eyesight.

Her mother sat there impatiently wishing San San would finish eating. "San San," she interrupted, "We have a nice surprise for you." Her father stepped out of the room and returned shortly with a brown package wrapped with string. He put it on the table.

San San put down the egg. She extended her fingers and carefully untied the string. She unwrapped the paper, folding it flat.

"A white silk blouse, for me?" San San exclaimed.

"Of course," her mother said.

San San ran her fingers lightly over the silk. She inhaled deeply, savoring the aroma. Her father smiled approvingly. His daughter always liked elegant things, like the camphor wood chest that had belonged to his grandmother. Her silk Pèi was still in it. He had seen his daughter open the chest, gaze at the Pèi, inhale deeply, then slowly close the chest. She had never asked about his grandmother, nor had he ever said anything about her. It was as if his daughter were savoring history by inhaling it.

San San held the blouse in front of her. "It's beautiful," she said, pulling it tightly against her breasts. She then slowly folded the blouse and laid it on the paper wrapping.

How like a child and an adult she was, her mother thought, and the red eggs? Were they not

like her ovaries, ripe and ready?

"San San," her mother began awkwardly. "You remember my brother Yuan Chung." San San shook her head. "That's right you were only three when he left for America. Well, anyway, he owns a gas station in San Francisco, and he has a friend he works with who owns a laundry and..."

San San looked at her mother who was clutching a letter in her hands. "Well, it says here that his friend wants to marry a nice Chinese girl from the mainland and my brother suggested you." Her mother said this quickly, never once looking at the letter as if holding it gave her words power.

San San's mind went blank. Was she hearing correctly? An arranged marriage? In this day and age?

"San San listen to me," her mother said. "Two months ago, you graduated from Sun Yat-Sen

University and you are only working in a department store. Yes, there will be promotions or other jobs, but here is an opportunity to go to America, to have a better life."

A better life? She was happy where she was. And what of her boyfriend Ling Chiao? Their plans? Their love-making? She looked at her father for help, but he seemed resigned to the wish of his strong-willed wife.

It was as if another mouth had formed the words, but San San found herself saying "Yes, Mother, I will go." San San did not know why she said this, but she said it.

She felt a knot in her stomach. Perhaps she really did want to set off on an adventure.

3

It had all happened so fast. The Air China flight approached San Francisco. San San sat in a seat next to the window and behind the wing. She could see the lights of the city, twinkling below. The couple in front of her were speaking English. She strained to understand them for she had taken four years of English at the university, but at times their words were just a murmur in the night. The woman next to her was asleep, her hands still clutching a magazine she had been reading. San San felt completely alone. What was her boyfriend Ling Chiao doing now? And her parents? Tears ran down her cheeks. Why had she left? What was in store for her?

San San sat in the back of the yellow cab speeding toward San Francisco. There was so much traffic, and the buildings seemed like blocks, cold and indifferent, unlike Hong Kong which for all its faults was warm and human. She was surprised when they reached Chinatown. Surprised at the surging crowds, the buildings with slopping tiled roofs and pagodas, and so many signs with Chinese characters. The cab driver had the window down. San San could hear the staccato of conversations in Cantonese.

Now she was here, in an alleyway in San Francisco's Chinatown, with an unknown man who was going to be her husband. That man, Geary Quan, opened the door to the apartment which was next to the laundry. San San followed him, taking apprehensive mincing steps. He turned on the light and pointed to an open door. She saw a bed, next to it was a little table with a lamp.

Against one wall was a dresser. Against another was a chest of drawers.

"That's yours," Geary said proudly pointing to the dresser which was made of unfinished pine.

An equally plain unpainted chair was in front of the dresser. Just above the dresser a dusty mirror hung on the wall. "I bought it for you." He said this in such atrocious Cantonese that she could barely understand him.

"Perhaps my dialect is different than yours. Maybe if we speak English," San San said. He repeated himself in English. It was not much better than his Cantonese, but she could not bear to hear such bad Cantonese, especially from someone she was going to have to live with.

"I own this place," he said smiling proudly and extending both hands. A laundry with an attached small apartment... he was boasting about this?

"You must be very proud," she said, trying her best to sound impressed.

"Now we go to bed," he said abruptly. San San was totally taken aback. No getting to know each other, no preliminaries, no romance.

"First I need to go to the bathroom." She felt embarrassed saying this, but she was holding her thighs tightly together in her discomfort.

"That room," he said, pointing.

As she sat on the toilet, she kept nervously clenching her toes until she was finished, then she stayed in the bathroom just to be still and to be by herself. It was too soon when she opened the door.

Was she seeing things? There he was, a naked chubby man with an erect penis that was much smaller than her boyfriend's. She wanted to run out the door. But where could she run to? Who did she know?

"I'm on my period," she said truthfully but also hoping it would put him off.

"So, that way you will not be pregnant."

Pregnant? She did not want to get pregnant by him, ever. Yes, thankfully she was on her period, and when she wasn't she definitely would be prepared.

San San felt embarrassed undressing in front of this strange man. She did not look at him, but she felt his eyes on her. She quickly climbed onto the bed, pulled the covers over her and lay there on her back. Suddenly he was on top of her. Her thighs accommodated him unwillingly.

She hardly felt his penis. Was this because it was smaller than Ling Chiao's? Because she was on her period? Or because her mind was numbing her body? His movements were mechanical, with no rhythm. Her body felt no response. He had a feeble orgasm, then rolled off her. He now lay next to her, snoring. San San felt completely isolated. Why had her parents sent her here? Why had she agreed? Where was Ling Chiao now?

She thought back to the last time she had seen him. They were hiking up to Bai Yun Lake. He stopped for a rest, or was it her? Suddenly she had gotten this wild impulsive idea. She plucked a flower growing by the side of the trail. San San touched Ling Chiao lightly on the chest, then reached down and unbuttoned his pants. His penis came flopping out. She tickled his penis with the flower, the whole time watching his heaving chest, until much to her delight and laughter his semen spurted over the flower and felt hot against her fingertips. Ling Chiao seemed confused as he buttoned up his pants. She merely smiled, dropped the flower, wiped her hands on her handkerchief, and put her hand in his. They continued hiking in silence.

How could she have been so frivolous? Was this the part of her that had hastily said "yes" to her mother's arranged marriage? She was afraid it was, and she was afraid of where it might lead her.

4

San San felt a cold chill. She reached down to pull the covers back over her. Where were they? She sat up. The covers had been pulled off her and were crumpled up at the foot of the bed. Through the door she could see a light on in the kitchen. So this was Geary's way of waking her up. She lay there wishing she were in her own bed in her parent's house. Just then Geary came in.

"It's six o'clock, dress, I have to go to work. There are your clothes," Geary pointed. On the floor there were several stacks of clothes all neatly folded. There was a stack of jeans, next to it were stacks of sweaters, skirts, underwear and socks, then a couple of pairs of shoes.

"Customers left these. After eight weeks I claim," Geary said proudly. "You take what fits, you can use the bottom three drawers."

"Dress in jeans and a sweater for work," Geary said, then he went back into the kitchen. San San was surprised to find that most of the clothes were almost new. She soon found a pair of jeans and a sweater that suited her.

Geary lay four strips of bacon in the frying pan. "Here, this is how to cook bacon," he said to San San as she came into the kitchen. San San had learned how to cook from her mother, and her aunt. It seemed rudimentary to her as she watched the strips sizzle in the frying pan. "You cook it till it's crisp, not too much on one side." San San took the fork out of his hands, impatient that any man would even think of telling her how to cook. He brought his plate over and she put the bacon strips on it. "Now the eggs," he said. He cracked open two eggs and fried them in the bacon grease. "See, sunny side up," he said proudly, as he slipped the spatula underneath them, and put them on the plate. Geary took two glasses from the dish rack on the sink. He opened the refrigerator and took out a carton of orange juice and filled both glasses. "Here," Geary said lifting his glass and taking a sip. "This is an American breakfast; I am very American. Drink. Drink like me." San San did not want to drink out of the glass because she could see grease spots. Reluctantly she drank. "You are very Chinese," he said. "Your name is San San. I give you an American name. Anne. You are Anne."

She was? He could give her a new name, just like that?

"Say it."

"Anne," she said.

"Sounds too much like 'Tan'. Try again."

"Anne," she said again.

"Good."

Geary took another plate out of the dish rack and put a piece of bacon on it from his plate and one egg. "This is an American breakfast. This is the breakfast I eat. But for dinner I prefer Chinese," he added. Anne looked around for chopsticks. "No, this you eat with a knife and fork." Geary said. Anne was famished. Still she restrained herself. She would eat like a lady, but she did not feel like eating with that large fork, especially one that said U.S. Navy on the handle.

"Here is your key," Geary said, reaching into his pocket. "I'll show you the laundry before I go to work." As they stepped out into Stark Alley, the cold morning air pierced right through her. She saw a white man asleep on a doorstep at the end of the alleyway. How could he stand it? How could he live? There was a sign to the right of the laundry door written in faded Chinese characters: "The Quan Shang Laundry." "You try," Geary said as they stood in front of the door. Anne put the key in and turned the handle. Nothing. "First, turn the key to the left." Geary instructed. Anne turned the key to the left, turned the handle, and the door opened.

"Here's the light switch," Geary said as he turned a switch on a panel to the right of the door.

The laundry was smaller than Anne had expected. It was, however, well laid out. For instance, in each space for the dryers, there was a dryer on the bottom and another one on top, and the washers were well laid out to manage the space they used. This could also be said for the folding tables.

Geary opened a door which was on the opposite side of the wall of their apartment. "This is the counter," he said as he rolled up a partition separating the counter from the rest of the laundry. The partition rolled up much like a roll top desk. "The front door key also fits the bathroom door in the back; and it opens the door inside the bathroom which leads to the apartment." Anne saw a sign above the door in Chinese characters: For Customers Only. She was glad to know the inner door also led into their apartment for that meant the house had an extra bathroom.

Geary pulled another smaller key out of his pocket. "This is for the counter drawer," he said, opening it. Inside were some bills and change. "There is the change machine," Geary said pointing to it on the wall, "and a list of phone numbers." Next to the phone was piece of paper and written in characters were plumber, washing machine repairman et cetera. Next to them were the corresponding phone numbers. "Customers will leave you clothes for washing and folding and for dry cleaning which we send out." Geary quickly looked at his watch. "I am late. You are open now." Geary hurried out the door without even bothering to kiss her or give her a last lingering look.

It was just as well. Anne was glad to see him go. Now she could be by herself. Hardly five minutes had passed when a Chinese woman with a strong peasant's physique came bustling in the door with her laundry cart almost overflowing. She flipped open the tops of several washers with a bang and began to stuff in her laundry. As soon as she had put the soap in and fed the machines with quarters, she banged down the lids of the washing machines. "Please go easy," Anne asked.

"Who are you?" the woman demanded in shrill Cantonese.

"I am..." Anne didn't know quite what to say for at this point she was not yet Mrs. Quan, and she did not want to say, "Geary Quan's girlfriend."

"Let me guess," the woman said quite quickly. "You are the new wife?" Anne shook her head. "Girlfriend?" Anne shook her head again. "Then you are the suck-suck girl," the woman said pulling her finger in her mouth and biting it provocatively. Anne's eyes grew wide. She had never heard such language before, especially coming from an older woman. She stood there numbly, not knowing whether to laugh or cry. Suddenly the woman threw her arms around Anne and said, "I like you anyway." Anne loved her warm embrace even if it did seem a bit rude. The woman held her in a mothering embrace, then unexpectedly dropped her arms and went back to her wash. "Yes, suck-suck, that what all the men want these days. I suck-suck, at least I won't get a disease. And you?" Anne blushed. "That's okay honey. It's your business, but I know, I know. By the way I am Mrs. Teng, and you?"

"Anne."

"So soon an American name for a nice Chinese girl. Well. Well, soon you be Mrs. Anne Quan." Anne started to say something but Mrs. Teng cut right in. "Geary said he was going to send for a wife. It is two weeks until the American New Year. Taxes, he has to marry before then." Anne wanted to stop her ears. Mrs.

Teng walked over and put her hand on Anne's shoulder. "It's okay. But it is best to be realistic." Anne felt a warm glow. In spite of this woman's being straightforward in a way that she had never experienced, Anne liked her.

The door opened and a stately Chinese woman entered carrying her clothes in a Gump's bag.

"Shhh," Mrs. Teng said putting her finger to her lips. "No more bad talk. It's Mrs. Sheh." The woman put the bag on the counter and said in Mandarin, "I would like these clothes dry cleaned." Anne, who had taken both English and Mandarin in school, responded in Mandarin though with a Cantonese accent. The woman gave her a condescending look.

There was a stack of notepad paper and a pen on the counter. "Name and address?" Anne asked.

"Mrs. Sheh." She then gave an address on the very outskirts of Russian Hill near Chinatown. Anne removed each piece of clothing from the Gump's bag and labeled them.

Mrs. Sheh watched Anne writing the Chinese characters. "I learned better in Peking, but not bad for nowadays. Certainly, better than the last girl could do. You should use an abacus when adding the bill. It's the only proper way." With that Mrs. Sheh took her receipt and walking in tune with some inaudible Strauss waltz walked out the door.

"You sure surprised her," Mrs. Teng said.

"How?" Anne asked.

"When you knew Mandarin."

"Well, I do, but no so well."

"Don't be so humble. Anyway, I know her. If you didn't know Mandarin, she was going to look at you like you were some lowly peasant from the south, sigh, then talk to you in Cantonese. Aristocratic lady condescends to speak the language of the peasants, and an abacus? Big show for tourists here in Chinatown. Russian Hill lady, huh, too good for suck-suck. Too good for hot sex. Then husband play."

"Mrs. Teng," Anne implored.

"Okay, I calm down. Not good for my heart anyway. Do you know the prices?"

Anne shook her head.

"I'll show you." Mrs. Teng stepped up to the counter and wrote the price on a label of each garment that Mrs. Sheh had left. Then Mrs. Teng made a list of the prices the laundry charged for dry cleaning and different items of clothing.

"Geary should have done this for you."

"So true," Anne said to herself.

Just then a tall white man wearing a Navy pea coat and watch cap pushed open the door with a bang. He quickly went over to a laundry basket, swung a seabag off his shoulder and let it flop into the basket. He walked over to the counter, wrote his name on a piece of paper, pulled out $20, then left, banging the door behind him.

Anne was surprised that a white person would come to the Quan Shang Laundry. After all it was in the heart of Chinatown.

"Alex Ivanoff. Lives in North Beach near here. No wash-fold there for sure. His father was a Cossack, you know." Anne shook her head. "Alex works with my nephew Shue Lee. Longshoreman. Big pay day. Write the character for "big" on his ticket. Now you can wash and fold just like me."

"Soon I go," Mrs. Teng said as she put her clothes in the dryer. "I think you know pretty good now."

Anne dumped the contents of the seabag out into the laundry basket. She was surprised at how greasy the clothes were. She walked behind the counter. There were several boxes of detergent. "Use plenty," Mrs. Teng advised as Anne put the clothes into the washers.

A half-hour later Mrs. Teng left. Anne almost cried. A friend. A friend. How she needed a friend.

As Anne lay in bed that night she felt a clammy hand cup her breast. Her skin tightened. Her eyes narrowed. Now she felt his weight on her. Did he think she was a sack? She tasted his tongue in her mouth. She knew his penis was inside her, but thankfully she hardly felt it. Just to get rid of him she reached down and tickled his testicles. That did it. She pushed him off her gently. Actually, she felt like shoving him off her, but she feared he would act like an enraged monkey being pushed away by his mother. Anne kissed the back of her hand, wishing it were Ling Chiao's. Sex that night had been no more satisfying than the first.

The next morning, she would find solace in the laundry where the days passed until soon they were more than she wished.

5

It was in the summer of '49 that a Chinese junk anchored off the Battery Street Wharf in San Francisco. A rowboat brought the prospective argonauts ashore. They were met with stares and jeers. No one had seen a Chinese before. No sooner had their curiosity worn off than the Forty-Niners were back in the saloons and tent brothels. Everyone it seemed was on their way to the gold fields and what time there was to waste was for having fun.

As they headed for the gold fields men scattered. Some following a rumor here, and another one there. Others just tagged along. Shang Quan and three of his countrymen followed, serving first as cooks and washermen for a few miners headed for the Auburn Ravine, and then moving on and becoming miners themselves. They got lucky. But as anti-Chinese sentiment began to grow, their claims were jumped and most of their gold stolen. Shang Quan headed back to San Francisco with a little gold which he had buried. It was not the fortune he had once had, but it was enough to send for a wife and to open a laundry. Miners had money, card sharks had money, bartenders and prostitutes had money, but the Quan Shang Laundry saw little of it.

Shang Quan saw his second chance when the Central Pacific railroad began hiring Chinese. They were paid little and because of the company store system it was hard to save. Still with his wife and son running the laundry he had a nest egg when the Transcontinental Railroad was completed and also enough to send for a wife for his son. In early 1906 Shang Quan died, then his wife. His son carried on in the same dilapidated building until the fire and earthquake of April 1906.

Wang Quan had always been angry with his father for converting what little savings they had into gold coins and hoarding them in a strongbox in the basement. "Why not put them in the bank. Think of the interest," he kept telling his father. But as he uncovered the strongbox amidst the smoldering ruins he silently thanked his father. There were not as many gold coins as he remembered. Had he imagined there were more? Had his father gambled some of them away or spent them on women? There were enough gold coins however to build a new laundry and send to China for a wife for his son.

Geary Quan, the great-grandson, owned the laundry and the building. If he sold the building that would make him a rich man, but then he would have to buy or rent someplace and that would make him a poor one.

Repairs and upkeep on the building were expensive, not to mention the water bill for the laundry. The laundry made a profit, but it was not what one might expect. Geary Quan's job at Pacific Auto Care station did not pay much. He saved what he could, but there were times, like when he had a roofing bill for $20,000 or when the main water heater had to be replaced, that he had to borrow from the bank and had nothing left.

6

It had been a month since Anne had become Mrs. Quan. They had been married at city hall. Afterwards Geary had gone back to work at Pacific Auto Care, and Anne had returned to the laundry. Geary's sexual techniques on their wedding night were still quick and abrupt. Their lives had now settled into a routine.

It was ten o'clock when the last customer left the Quan Shang Laundry. Anne locked the door and went into the storage room. Soon she was mopping the floor. She enjoyed cleaning the laundry, making it just like new. She was singing softly to herself. Geary Quan stood at a folding table counting the money. He sorted the pennies, nickels, dimes, and quarters into piles, then counted and stuffed them into the paper cylinders that he got from the Bank of America. He marked down the amount of each roll on a yellow piece of paper. If he was not going to use a calculator, Anne thought, why not let her do it? No, he did not think it was her place.

Suddenly he shouted, "Not much money. Not much money." She paid little attention to him. Some days and weeks were bad, and some were good. Anyway, they were making more now that he had before she came, and she knew it was partly because customers enjoyed talking to her.

He walked up and stood in front of her. "Not much money. Not much money," he shouted. She looked at his bloated face. Had he been drinking again? God, she found him disgusting.

"Look." He spread out the Sing Tao Daily newspaper that they had left out for their customers to read. She looked over the newspaper, feeling superior, knowing that there were many characters that he did not know. The page contained mostly ads for waitresses, cooks, seamstresses, grocery clerks, things like that. He pointed to the bottom of the page. It said "Blossom Wong's The House of Delirious Harmony. Elegant Massage Girl wanted." She looked at him puzzled, perhaps he had not understood the characters.

"I phoned already," he said, starting to smile. "Part-time girl is okay." He repeated this as if being a part-time massage girl made it any less than what it really was, a prostitute with a fancy title. He put his hand on her shoulder. "A few days a month we get three or four hundred extra," he said.

Was she dreaming? So this is what her arranged marriage had come to: a husband who was so greedy that he would even let his own wife work as a massage girl. For the moment she could not even think of the word "prostitute" though she knew that was what she would be.

Geary refolded the newspaper, put the rolls of coins in the money drawer behind the counter, and left for their apartment. Anne continued cleaning the laundry. She must have spent an extra hour or more polishing the machines and mopping the floor.

Anne opened the door to their bedroom. She saw him lying in bed asleep as if nothing had happened. She sat down on the couch to think and be by herself. She imagined that she was in the arms of Ling Chiao, her boyfriend in China. Soon she was dreaming: They were sitting by the Bai Yun Lake and Ling was caressing her breasts and kissing the nape of her neck and they were laughing together in a way she and her husband never laughed.

She awoke late. The sun was streaming through the curtains. Geary had already left for his job as a mechanic at Pacific Auto Care. Anne remembered her dream. She kept savoring it, going over it as if watching a good scene in a movie again and again. If only last night were a dream and Ling Chiao the reality of her life.

Anne unlocked the front door of the laundry. Although she had risen late for her, it was only eight o'clock. One of her favorite customers Tammy and her lively little girls were waiting with a huge cart stuffed with laundry. Anne propped open the door with an old wedge-shaped piece of wood. She took two net shopping bags from behind the counter and started walking down Stockton Street. Stockton Street was the heart of Chinatown. Thankfully there weren't the crowds of tourists that were on Grant Avenue. The shop signs were mostly written in Chinese characters and Cantonese could be heard everywhere. Some people spoke Mandarin and English was seldom spoken except to white customers.

As she passed Pacific Street several policemen were on their bicycle patrol. One of them whose blond hair and white skin contrasted sharply with his black uniform waved to her. Anne smiled and began to walk more gingerly.

Why couldn't her husband smile when he saw her or the customers? Instead he always had a scowl and was usually in a black mood.

Anne could hear children laughing and the sound of a basketball being dribbled behind her.

As she continued down Stockton Street Anne entered the Sun Sang Market. "Black mushrooms? Where are they?" she asked the clerk.

"In the back next to the bok choy," he replied.

A gray-headed Chinese woman dressed in a peasant's faded black jacket and trousers stood in front of the bin of black mushrooms picking them over and putting them into a crumpled paper bag. Anne wondered if the woman's hands were clean, and if it was necessary to be so picky. The woman talked to herself though very quietly. Only a few words here and there were understandable.

How different this woman was from her grandmother. Wei Min Peng had been on the Long

March, and had known Chairman Mao. Could she have had an affair with him? And if so, what was Anne's lineage? Her grandmother had seemed masculine to her when she was in China, her voice a little deeper than most women's, her stance more military-like. But now that Anne was living in the United States, her grandmother merely seemed proud. The gray-headed woman picking over the black mushrooms was a reminder of what life been like before Mao. Except for the Cultural Revolution Chairman Mao had been right.

Anne wondered about herself. Here she was shopping, trying to cook a pleasing dish for her husband. Was she becoming like this traditionally dressed woman? True she rebelled in her mind, but was that enough?

There was not one person in the laundry when Anne returned. At times like this the quiet she experienced was like the quiet she experienced when she was the only one home in her parent's house, or like when out of curiosity she had gone into Saint Mary's Church on Grant Avenue. There was no mass. She sat in the back of the church and watched the flickering flames of the votive candles. She talked quietly to herself wishing for her life to change. This was her prayer.

It was seven o'clock when Anne finally pulled down the laundry counter shutter. The laundry itself would remain open until ten o'clock. In her spare time during the afternoon Anne had begun to prepare the evening meal and now there were only a few things left to do. As she stirred the rice she heard the door open. Her stomach felt heavy, and her hand grew leaden. He was home, and her body was tightening...

"Smells good," Geary said as he walked in with quick steps. He sat down without even washing his hands and began devouring his meal like one of her uncle's pigs. His head was bent so low that some of the strands of his hair were in the meal. While Anne could appreciate the fact that he might be hungry after a hard day's work, couldn't he hold back? Couldn't he restrain himself just a little? It was the same with sex, she reminded herself.

Geary leaned back in his chair and rocked it slightly backward, self-satisfied, as if he had accomplished something by gobbling down his meal.

He looked over at her. A slight smile crossed his face. She could tell that he liked her in her favorite black sweater and skirt. She sipped her tea. Their two teacups which he had inherited from his father were the only beautiful things they owned. Everything else was bland. The furniture, the dishes from Goodwill and the U.S. Navy utensils. She blew on her tea, cooling it.

Geary glanced at his watch. "Seven-thirty," he said in an alarmed tone of voice.

"So," she answered.

"Time to go."

Anne looked at him quizzically.

"Don't you remember? Blossom Wong's. Blossom Wong's tonight."

Anne's hands trembled. She clutched her teacup. It was precious to her though now she wished it weren't. So that was his thanks for her well-cooked meal. She knew what she should do. She should throw the tea in his face and walk out of the house. But to where? With what? She had no money except for her grocery allowance. He saw to that. Instead, she sat there silently and slowly put the teacup down.

Why couldn't she be more like her grandmother, and stand up to him instead of always accepting? What would happen? Maybe the worst that would happen would be better than this.

She heard him on the phone talking in his broken Cantonese. "Yes, Yes, Madame Wong, we're on our way." He hurried back into the room.

"Get ready. Get ready."

What was she supposed to do? Put on bright red lipstick like a prostitute? Maybe take a razor blade and slit her skirt up the sides?

He opened the front door. Why had he bothered to say, "Get ready?" Probably he didn't even know.

As they drove down Stockton Street she saw people in front of the stores. What would they think of her if they knew where she was going? What would her parents think?

Geary drove without saying a word, down Stockton Street, then down Bush. They waited at the stop light at Grant Avenue. Tourists and Chinese were milling about, going to stores and restaurants, and about their lives, and all seemed happy.

There was barely enough room for their pickup to pass as Geary turned into Quincy Alley. Geary parked the truck at the far end of the alley. Anne got out of the pickup. She looked up and down the alley. It was even worse than she had expected. The brick buildings were old and dilapidated, there were no stores and no signs of life. She looked up at a long black lacquered board affixed to the right side of a doorway. On it written in elegant gold Chinese characters was "The House of Delirious Harmony." Anne heard her husband backing up the pickup. She started to run after him, losing ground. She stopped in the middle of the alley. She turned around and walked back to Blossom Wong's. Hesitantly she stood on the step and knocked on the door.

A peephole opened and a stern eye looked out. "Name?" a heavy male voice asked in Cantonese. "Anne Quan," she answered. Anne smiled, this was too much like one of those gangster movies she had seen on T.V. The peephole shut and she could hear receding steps. Anne waited and waited. She was just about to walk away when the door opened. She stood there for a moment taking in the scene before her. There were dark wood paneled walls. On the walls were antique Chinese hanging scrolls and silk tapestries, mostly of beautiful landscapes. Along one wall, were some very old antique carved chairs and low antique tables.

The most stunning Chinese women Anne had ever seen sat in those chairs. She knew from her schoolbooks and the museums she had been to in China that these furnishings must have cost a mint. She knew too that such women did not come cheap.

Standing to her left stood a large thick-set Chinese man dressed in a dark double-breasted suit with faint pinstripes. This was undoubtedly the man who had looked out the peephole.

A woman with black hair with gray streaks walked toward her. Anne guessed her to be about fifty, but she could have been older. Her face was free of wrinkles or any blemishes. She probably had used some traditional Chinese lotions on her face in the past, and nowadays some very expensive modern ones. She wore a gold silk embroidered Pèi. One could certainly not find one like it in any shop nowadays. Anne wondered where she had gotten it.

The woman extended her hand and said in very aristocratic Cantonese, "Welcome, San San Quan. My name is Blossom Wong, I am so pleased that you have come." Anne also extended her hand, touching Blossom Wong's fingertips. She found herself bowing slightly. Blossom Wong observed Anne visualizing what kind of Qípáo would suit her. "Please remember," she said, "that outside you may be Mrs. Anne Quan, but here you are always San San."

Anne looked around, savoring the decor, and fascinated by the beautiful women sitting in the ornately carved chairs. One was reading a Chinese novel. Another was reading a Chinese fashion magazine. Another was polishing her nails. All of them wore Qípáos and had a classical beauty that appeared to be lifted from Shanghai in the 30's. They seemed to be sizing her up and indeed she heard one of them whisper to another, "New girl, perhaps some competition." Anne stood there feeling out of place in her skirt and sweater. Blossom Wong started walking in very slow measured steps. Anne followed and was surprised at how lush the carpet felt beneath her feet. They passed an oak door that looked like it led to the board room of a bank. "That is my room," Blossom Wong said. "Feel free to knock if you need me." They turned into a narrow hallway. There were several doors. "You may wish to take a shower dear," Blossom Wong said in a quiet commanding voice. "Always, before and after," she added.

"Before and after?" How Anne wished she had not heard these words. Before and after customers, strangers who would pay for sex. As Anne stepped forward Blossom Wong observed her walk thinking how elegant she would look in her Qípáo. "Take as long as you like dear," Blossom Wong said as Anne started to undress.

Anne felt the tingle of warm water against her body. There was a plastic bottle of lavender soap. Anne poured some on her hands, smelled it, then rubbed it on her arms and breasts. She put her head back enjoying the spray against her face and the sound of it against the tiles. Suddenly she realized that she had forgotten to wash her vagina. She shouldn't be naive about what she was getting into. She started soaping her pubic hair. Sex was why she was here. She may as well face the truth.

After almost an hour Anne pulled back the shower curtain and stepped out. As she reached for a towel she noticed that her clothes were neatly folded and put on top of a towel on a chair except for her bra, panties, and shoes, and that a dark green Qípáo was on the hanger where her clothes had been. Anne ran her hands over the silk. She wondered how much the Qípáo had cost. But that certainly was no problem here.

Anne slid into the Qípáo. It felt wonderful against her skin. She walked over to a full-length mirror. Was she the woman who looked back at her? The woman in the mirror looked like a high-class mistress from Shanghai. What was there to do but refine the picture? There was an elegant dresser against the wall on which were several brushes, combs, lipsticks, and jars of make-up. Most of them had French names and were beyond her means. The dresser had been well stocked for Blossom Wong's girls. Anne combed out her hair and put on dark red lipstick. She laughed as she saw her reflected image. She had to admit she enjoyed looking at herself.

Just then there was a light knock on the door. "May I come in?" Blossom Wong asked. Anne felt that this was a question to which she could have said, "No," but she was as ready as she would ever be. "Yes," Anne answered. Blossom Wong opened the door, then quietly closed it. She looked at Anne approvingly but said nothing.

"Perhaps I should explain a few things," Blossom Wong said quietly. "There are light switches in each room, one right above the other. The top one is for the light which is purposely quite dim. The bottom one is in case you have trouble with a customer. Press it down and you will shortly have assistance. I want to assure you that we very seldom have trouble in a place like this. Oh, and another thing, when you are finished be sure to put $100 under my door. You need not bother to clean up your room. We have other people for that. Here's some prophylactics for your use." Anne took them shyly, almost like a schoolgirl. Blossom Wong reached out and held Anne's hand for a moment. "Come out when you are ready dear."

Anne looked at herself again in the mirror. "Well, Blossom Wong approved and so should I." Anne walked to the door and opened it. Her hand felt sweaty as she turned the handle.

There were several empty chairs in the parlor. Anne chose the one farthest from the front door. Even so she felt conspicuous as she leaned back and wrapped her fingers around the ends of the arms of the chair on which were ornately carved dragons. The other girls, she noticed, were sitting there quite casually as if they were in their own living rooms. One was still reading a Chinese fashion magazine, another was drinking tea, another continued buffing her nails. Though none of them seemed to be paying any attention to her still she felt they were casting glances at her and sizing her up. The woman sipping tea whispered something to the woman buffing her nails. She stopped briefly, rocked her head back, covered a laugh with her hand, and continued buffing her nails. Had they talked about her? She thought she caught the words, "New girl... so beautiful." Next to her was a small table on which were some Chinese and American fashion magazines. Anne picked up a copy of Vogue. She thumbed through the pages. She loved the ads, especially the Coco Chanel ones. She started to read an article on the gardens of Florence.

Someone knocked on the door. She saw the thickset bouncer in his ominous dark suit walk silently toward the door. He looked out of the peephole, then motioned Blossom Wong over. She stood on tiptoes then nodded. The bouncer unlocked and unbolted the door, then slowly opened it. An elegant Chinese man with receding gray hair, wearing a well-tailored suit with a carnation entered. Although he stood tall and erect, he had a cane inlaid with mother of pearl. It certainly suited him. He bowed slightly and kissed the back of Blossom Wong's hand. "I see that you are still that beautiful Shanghai girl out for some fun," he said playfully as he pinched her cheek. Anne could see him eyeing the girls while pretending to admire the decor. "Yes, yes. This place looks much like the one you had in Shanghai."

"Yan Yun, darling," Blossom Wong said softly. "Mr. Zhou needs to be escorted to his room." The woman who had been buffing her nails stood up. She was a little taller than Anne had at first thought. She smiled at Mr. Zhou as if she had known him all her life. She walked slowly, voluptuously, in her Qípáo. Soon she was laughing at something Mr. Zhou had said.

Anne returned to reading the Vogue article on the gardens of Florence. The accompanying photos were absolutely beautiful. She was wondering where Fiesole was when she felt a light tap on her shoulder. She looked up and saw the smiling face of Blossom Wong. Standing behind Blossom Wong was a man who smiled apprehensively. He was a little on the short side for her taste, but he was well dressed. There was not much more she could tell about him. "Mr. Choong wishes to meet you dear," Blossom Wong said. Anne stood up. Mr. Choong was even shorter than she thought. "Anne, this is Mr. Choong. Big shot here in Chinatown," Blossom Wong laughed. Anne stood there, not knowing what to say. She smiled and pretended to be impressed. Behind her she heard one of the girls snicker. "Perhaps you can take Mr. Choong to room four. It's down the hallway and up to your left." With that Blossom Wong walked away.

Anne walked in front of Mr. Choong toward room four. She felt self-conscious in her Qípáo. She had to take the stairs slowly, but she certainly was in no hurry. When she reached the landing, she stopped for a second. She could hear him wheezing as he climbed the stairs. Only four stairs and out of breath already? Fat and out of shape. Just the kind of man she hated. Definitely not like her Ling Chiao, he with the tapered body of a snow leopard and a hot sexual appetite with control. Did she have to... did she have to do this? How could her husband think of such a thing?

Anne turned the handle of the door. Damn, why wasn't it locked? There was a small statue of the Buddha on a night table, a bathtub with a shower and a low bed which was actually a large futon on a raised platform. White sheets covered the futon. There were several folded towels and extra sheets at the foot of the bed.

Anne turned around. She looked down on Mr. Choong's short pudgy body. What would it look like naked? Ugly. He stood there smoothing his hair, calming himself. He looked at her breasts heaving from nervousness. His eyes searched her body, imagining what her public hair was like. Very hairy he hoped.

"You have nice feet," he said.

Anne blushed. Nice feet. What was this?

"Could you take off your shoes?" he said hesitantly.

Take off her shoes? Well, she was going to have to remove her clothes sooner or later anyway.

She braced herself by putting her right hand against the wall. She slipped off her shoes.

"May I see?" he asked very politely.

Anne raised her right foot. But she could not raise it very high because she was not used to the Qípáo.

"That's okay." Mr. Choong said. He started to kneel down. Now he was on his knees. He touched her toes, running his fingers over them.

"My mother had bound feet," he said.

How old was his mother? Or he for that matter? Bound feet? She had almost forgotten that Chinese women ever had them. Besides, what did that have to do with her?

"And so did my grandmother," he added.

Suddenly he started nibbling on her toes, then licking in between them. Anne found this pleasant enough much to her surprise. He then lifted her right foot gently and began sucking on each toe, almost like a woman going down on a man's penis for she could see his head bob slightly. He tickled her little toe with his tongue, then started on the other foot.

Suddenly he stopped. He stood up. "Now you do me," he said. Do him? Lick and suck his toes? The thought of it made her sick.

"I charge three hundred dollars for feet," she said, thinking that if she set such a high price, he would forget about it.

He sat down on the chair and wiped the perspiration from his face. Was he really that out of shape? He reached back and pulled out a wallet fat with bills. He handed three one hundred dollars bills as if he were handing her three dollars. She should have known that at Blossom Wong's three hundred dollars was nothing.

He bent over and started to untie his shoes. "Could you help me?" he asked. Anne nodded and said, "Yes." Now she was on her knees, taking off his shoes then his socks wondering what her mother would think.

He began undressing, folding his clothes neatly in the chair. Suddenly his fat naked body was before her. He kissed her hand and lay down on the futon.

"My mother had bound feet," he repeated. "You've heard of the sixty-nine? Same position only this is the twenty-toes," he said. Anne nodded. "We suck each other's toes, now get undressed."

Anne looked at the statue of the Buddha. Although she was not religious, she asked for help.

"Sure," she said. "Sure," as if she were quite used to this.

"Just a minute," she said thinking quickly and partly playing for time. She stepped over to the towel rack near the tub. She grabbed a wash rag and turned on the hot water. She wrang it out and brought it over with a towel. She proceeded to wash and inspect his feet. There was a bunion on his right big toe. There was fungus between two of his toes. And worse yet his feet stank. No amount of washing was going to change this. Why her? Why?

Anne stood up, her eyes avoiding his erect penis. "I want to brush my teeth," she said. "I have to get my toothbrush." She did not wait for an answer. She walked out to the parlor. Two of the girls giggled when they saw her. She knocked on Blossom Wong's door.

Blossom Wong opened it. A Chinese opera was on the television, and she seemed upset that she was being disturbed. Anne handed her a hundred-dollar bill. Blossom Wong put it on the table. Anne thanked her and closed the door, wishing she could have stayed and watched the Chinese opera.

"Customer wants noodles," Anne said to Blossom Wong's girls who were chatting and whispering among themselves, as she quickly opened the door and stepped out into Quincy Alley. She knew that if she had waited even a second, one of the girls would have said, 'That's okay," and phoned a Chinese restaurant for a take-out order, and indeed one of them had started to reach for the phone. Anne imagined them talking among themselves, "New girl, doesn't know any better."

As soon as she had stepped outside into Quincy Alley Anne realized she had forgotten her shoes. But she was not going back. Now she could feel a chill from the cold fog penetrating through her Qípáo. Still, the fog caressed her softly the way she wished her husband would caress her, the way Ling Chiao had caressed her. She soon found that if she walked in a certain way, raising and lowering her feet gently that she would not scrape them against the sidewalk. Anne liked walking this way. It was after all not much different than the way she normally walked.

The smells from the restaurants along Grant Avenue floated into her nostrils. An aroma, where was it from, made her feel like she was in her mother's kitchen. Grant Avenue was crowded with tourists and Chinese all seemingly in a hurry. All that was needed were rickshaws to complete a picture of Shanghai or Hong Kong in the 30's. She even heard a man whose voice sounded as if he were from her hometown. She looked, but the voice quickly faded. Had she imagined it?

Anne turned up the Pine Street hill. She saw a De Soto cab. Should she hail it? She certainly could afford it. She had $200 in the red silk purse with the embroidered green dragon that her mother given her for her fifteenth birthday. No, she would save her money. She did not hail the cab. A black Lincoln town car driven by a chauffeur slowed down, then stopped. An elegant looking Japanese man sat in the back. The front electric window went down. The chauffeur leaned over and said, "Ride miss?" Anne started to say "No," but suddenly she found herself walking toward the town car. The rear door opened, she hesitated, then stepped inside.

As she sat down, she was surprised to see the Japanese man looking out the other window away from her. After a few minutes he spoke to the driver in Japanese in a quiet yet authoritative tone of voice.

Anne leaned back enjoying the comfort and the smell of fine leather. And as long as he was looking out the window on his side, she thought she may as well look out hers. There was an old Chinese woman with a baby on her back, a young couple holding hands and tourists, lots of tourists, nothing unusual. She felt his eyes on her. She turned toward him and was surprised to see that his face though clean shaven had the stubble of a beard. Was this unusual in Japanese men? she wondered. She liked it. He looked so much more masculine than her husband.

He smiled at her then very slowly said, "Miss, I do not speak English very well. And certainly no Chinese," he added with a laugh.

"And I speak no Japanese," she replied.

The town car continued out Pine Street passing people and buildings Anne no longer cared about. She simply sank into the leather upholstery wishing she could remain in this luxury forever. She soon fell asleep sinking more deeply into the soft leather.

Anne awoke with a start when the door opened. She looked for her traveling companion, but he was gone. The chauffeur held the door open. In Cantonese-accented English he said, "Mr. Okamoto said you may go to his room if you wish miss." She nodded her head. As Anne stepped out, she recognized the Hotel Kabuki though she had never expected to see the inside of it.

She followed the chauffeur to the door. He opened it and stood there stiffly as she entered. Anne felt as if all eyes were on her. With her green Qípáo and her willowy figure she certainly was one of the more elegant women to have entered the hotel that week. In her mind people were staring at her bare feet. The desk clerk looked her over, pretending to be looking in the reservation book. A couple of gentlemen who were conversing paused for breath. A gorgeous redhead with ample cleavage in the tow of a middle-aged businessman fixed her eyes on Anne, then looked away as if she hadn't noticed her or wished Anne didn't exist. Her escort smiled at Anne until the redhead tugged on his arm.

Anne followed the chauffeur who walked very authoritatively. She now noticed that he had a more muscular build than was at first apparent. Probably he knew some form of martial arts and was undoubtedly carrying a gun. He pressed the elevator button. As the door opened a man who looked like a linebacker stepped out. He almost bumped into Anne. The chauffeur grabbed the man's wrist which took advantage of the man's forward momentum and propelled him out into the lobby.

The elevator doors closed. The chauffeur looked straight ahead as if Anne didn't exist. Time seemed frozen as they passed floor after floor. Finally, the elevator doors opened.

The chauffeur stepped out. Anne followed his quick, sure steps. He stopped suddenly, put his ear to a door, then opened it; Anne stepped in. She heard the door shut behind her. She turned around, but the chauffeur had not come in. Anne looked around the room. There was beautiful origami on the dresser. She saw no sign of Mr. Okamoto. Then out of the corner of her eye she noticed his shoes on the floor near the head of the bed. She walked over to the closet. Curiously she opened it. His clothes were hung up neatly, even the underwear, a leather suitcase stood upright against the wall. Anne smiled at his fastidiousness and sense of simplicity. He probably wouldn't like her laundry much less her apartment.

Anne thought she heard something in the bathroom. Suddenly she felt very exuberant. She smiled as she pushed open the door. Mr. Okamoto sat in a rectangular tub, his back to her. He turned his head and looked at her as if he had expected her the whole while. Anne went back into the bedroom. She took off her Qípáo, her underpants and bra and hung them in the closet. Could she be doing this? Why not? Despite its classy appearance Blossom Wong's was after all a brothel. And even though she had done nothing there except have her toes sucked, Anne felt incredibly dirty, and besides she had walked on the sidewalk with her bare feet.

Anne adjusted the shower until it was slightly cool. She washed her feet feeling the dust slide off them, though when she looked at them, they did not seem that dirty. Besides she had sized Mr. Okamoto up and could tell he would not like dirt in the tub though he probably would not say anything.

As Anne walked toward the tub Mr. Okamoto held his breath. He had not expected her to be so lovely and sexy. She had taut breasts, shapely legs, and much more pubic hair than he had expected. Anne slowly lowered herself into the tub. Although she hardly knew Mr. Okamoto, she felt quite comfortable sitting in front of him. They looked into each other's eyes, seeking out the other's self. Mr. Okamoto smiled, then offered Anne the soap. Anne began rubbing the soap against her skin, with one hand then the other, washing herself in much the same manner as if Mr. Okamoto weren't there. Presently she found Mr. Okamoto's warm hands soaping her arms, then her breasts. He said something in Japanese. Although she did not understand him, she liked his soft, deep voice. She began soaping his shoulders then his back. She was surprised at how muscular he was. Had he been in the military? Or an athlete like her boyfriend? Anne thought of her boyfriend then quickly forgot about him. She reached down and almost unconsciously grabbed Mr. Okamoto's penis, stoking it until it was hard, then slipping it inside her. She continued soaping his back. Soon she felt his strong hands tightly but firmly against the back of her ribs as he too soaped her. He whispered something in her ear in Japanese, then rubbed his cheek against hers. Although she had seen it, she was surprised to feel stubble as she in turn rubbed her cheek against his face. As he spoke she heard the word "Ainu" then a slight laugh. What he had said was: "Maybe I have an Ainu ancestor." His belly now pressed against hers. Their bellies were now in sync, back and forth, faster and faster. She could feel his legs spasm. They clutched each other, then slowly parted. Although she did not have an orgasm, she felt a complete release in his.

He smiled at her, said something in Japanese, gently brushed his hand against her hair, then stood up and stepped out of the tub. Anne leaned back in the tub, stretching out her arms. This day had taken so many turns. First she was working in the laundry, then her husband had sent her to be a prostitute in a high-class brothel. Thank goodness for the man with the stinky feet, she thought, otherwise she wouldn't be here. Here she was being treated the way she wanted to be treated, the way her boyfriend Ling Chiao had treated her.

Anne turned her head. She could see Mr. Okamoto drying off. She swung her leg over the side of the tub. Her head felt light for a second as she stood up.

She reached for his towel and began drying him, as soon as she finished, she kissed his back. Whether he took this as some kind of signal or simply was tired, he took his bathrobe off the hanger, put it on, and walked out the door. Anne sat on the edge of the tub. She was happy to be alone with no cares for the moment. Twenty minutes passed, maybe more. Anne began to feel cold. She dried off, put on her Qípáo, and with a heavy heart walked out the door.

She smiled as she saw Mr. Okamoto lying in bed with the blankets pulled up almost over his head. She could hear him snoring, though very lightly. Anne felt like tucking herself in beside him, but she did not want to wake him; he must be very tired after his flight. As she started toward the door something made her stop. She wanted to see Mr. Okamoto again and again. How? She could wake him up and by signs get his business card. Or give him her address. But what if he didn't want to give it to her? Nor should she risk him coming to the laundry.

Anne felt like a thief in the night as she quietly opened the closet. His trousers were hanging up with the seams perfectly straight. She reached into the left hip pocket. Nothing. She tried the right one, again nothing. Her heart sank. She may as well try the coat. She reached into the right inside pocket. There it was, his wallet. She pulled it out and tiptoed into the bathroom. There were several one-hundred-dollar bills in it and a few twenties. She was not even tempted. She thumbed through the credit cards and... it must be these... five identical business cards printed with Japanese calligraphy. Certainly his business cards. She decided to take one, he probably wouldn't miss it, she hoped. She began to have doubts. Were these his business cards? Why weren't they in English? After all he was here in America on a business trip she presumed. Well, it was all she could find, so she better make the best of it. She was hardly going to risk ransacking his suitcase and waking him up. Besides he would get the wrong idea and think she was a hustler and a thief.

Anne carefully put the wallet back in the inside pocket of his coat. Miraculously she even remembered which side it had been in. He was still snoring as she quietly walked toward the door. Now that she had accomplished what she had wanted to accomplish she felt like waking him up with a kiss. *No*, she thought. *He probably has jet lag. Let him sleep.* Anne took one last look at what she could see of his face. She tried to drill it into her memory, for, after all, it might be the last time she would see him, then reluctantly she turned the handle of the door.

As Anne stepped out into the hallway she was surprised to see the chauffeur, and just to the right of the door, a new pair of black shoes. She stood there for a moment. The chauffeur said nothing, then hesitantly she stepped into the black shoes. They were a little tight, but she could easily have them stretched by the shoemaker. Anne waited for the chauffeur to lead her. He made no motion. Finally, Anne started toward the elevator and the chauffeur followed.

7

As Anne sat in the back of the town car her stomach felt heavy. She dreaded going back to the laundry. What she had experienced seemed like a dream. That dream though must be true otherwise she would not be riding in the back of a Lincoln town car dressed in a Qípáo and wearing a new pair of shoes. Her lover was sleeping and hopefully dreaming of her. She did not want to go back to her normal life. No.

"Where do you live miss?" the chauffeur asked.

"In Stark Alley just off Stockton Street." The chauffeur continued driving and Anne continued thinking of the hotel room and of Mr. Okamoto.

Suddenly the chauffeur pulled over and stopped on Stockton Street. Anne was shocked. She had to admit she was afraid of him. He could rape and kill her and no one would know the difference. "Miss," he began very slowly in Cantonese, "just a second." He pulled out a scrap of paper and a pen from his breast pocket. "Here is my phone number," he said. "If you ever have any trouble, please phone me." Anne suspected that this had been Mr. Okamoto's idea.

"Yes," Anne said, in an almost inaudible whisper as she looked at the number and put it in her purse.

"I may not be able to come right away. So leave a message if I'm out. I will come, but I have other jobs."

Other jobs? There was something sinister about the way he said this. She suspected that he was a member of the Chinese underworld and a gun for hire.

"We are only a few blocks from your house, miss." The chauffeur now got out of the town car, walked around and opened her door. Anne felt cold and nervous. She looked at her watch, it was 1 a.m.

"It is best that you be seen walking home," the chauffeur said. He was right about that, Anne thought. She would really have some explaining to do to Geary if she arrived with the chauffeur in the Lincoln town car.

"Don't worry. No harm will come to you." Anne started walking down Stockton Street. Though she did not turn her head she could feel him behind her. A few cars passed. There was no one else on the sidewalk. Why was the chauffeur following her like a daddy watching over his little girl on the way to school? Only a block to go. Anne picked up the pace. Suddenly a Jeep Cherokee pulled up with four Chinese teenagers in it. One of them rolled down the front window and shouted in Cantonese. "Hey, baby you want a ride. You want to try all of us. You got some nice lips." Anne paid no attention and acted as if she didn't hear. Now the Jeep Cherokee slowed down and came to a stop. Two of the teenagers got out. Anne's heart raced. Were these gang members trying to kidnap and rape her? She started to run. Just then she heard three shots. Anne turned around.

The chauffeur was gone. Two teenagers lay bleeding in the street. The Jeep Cherokee had a flat tire. The other teenagers were driving it anyway. As soon as it passed Anne turned back around. She walked half a block more, then breathed a sigh of relief as she turned into Stark Alley.

Anne could smell the aroma of whiskey as she entered the house. An open bottle of Jack Daniels was on the kitchen table. She looked in the bedroom. There he was sprawled out on top of the covers. Drinking again at the Club Hong Kong no doubt. Well, she certainly wasn't going to crawl into bed with him. Anne carefully took off her Qípáo and put it on a hanger. She slipped off her shoes. She smelled the leather. It reminded her of the smell of the leather in the town car and of elegance and refinement.

Anne put on her pajamas. She curled up on the couch. She held onto the cushion as if embracing Mr. Okamoto. Where was he? Where was he? For now, he seemed like a dream.

8

Anne awoke feeling cold. She should have gotten a blanket out of the linen closet. As she sat up and stretched her arms, she ran her fingers through her hair getting rid of any tangles before she combed it. The bedroom door was open, and Anne could see that her husband had left for his job as a mechanic at Pacific Auto Care.

Anne ate a quick breakfast of tea and cold rice. She carefully folded the Qípáo, then put it in a clean plastic bag. The delivery trucks were unloading on Stockton Street, which was already crowded with grocerymen and teamsters shouting at each other.

Two gray-headed women were picking over the melons on the stand in front of the Sun Sang Market. Anne could hear them say in Cantonese, "Too hard. Too hard." Anne turned down Sacramento Street. For a while she followed a little boy with a Mickey Mouse backpack holding his mother's hand. After a couple of blocks, they turned into the Hing Tai Le preschool. As Anne approached Grant Avenue, she saw several Chinese going to mass at Saint Mary's. Anne had gone to mass once in China. She felt that the Host could have germs and that communion was not a very sanitary practice.

With a heavy heart Anne turned into Quincy Alley. The weathered brick buildings remained indifferent to her footsteps. Finally she stood in front of The House of Delirious Harmony's door. She knocked. Silence. Did anyone hear? She knocked again. She started to walk away. Anne had heard stories about prostitutes who had been roughed up and worse, because they hadn't been straight with the house. Finally Anne knocked once more. Suddenly she heard Blossom Wong shout, "Go away, you horny toad. Go away. We open later."

"It's me, San San Quan," Anne yelled back. "I want to return the Qípáo. I will not be working here." Anne heard the bolt slide, the doorknob turned, then the door opened. Anne was surprised to see Blossom Wong in pajamas and a nightcap. Although she looked much older than when Anne had last seen her, she still seemed quite sprightly.

"Come in," Blossom Wong said. "Do come in." Anne entered. She was surprised to see no bouncer or anybody else for that matter.

"Here, have some tea dear. I was just serving myself." There was a teacup and a cup on the table in the parlor.

"I'll be right back," Blossom Wong said as she walked to her room, the backs of her slippers snapping against her heels. The parlor seemed lifeless in contrast to last night. In a corner Anne saw a large jade Buddha that she had not noticed the night before. She wondered how old the hanging scrolls and the tapestries were. The scrolls were probably older than the two scrolls her grandmother had had and they were a couple of hundred years old.

Blossom Wong returned with a teacup that was a match to the one on the table. Blossom Wong poured tea in both cups. She lifted her teacup then Anne lifted hers.

"You know," Blossom Wong began as if Anne had asked, "I had a place like this in Shanghai. I could see Mao's revolution coming, so in 1947 I came here."

Anne wondered how old Blossom Wong was. She certainly did not seem that old. As if Blossom Wong were reading her mind she said, "I've always taken herbs prescribed by my herbalist and I've always gone to the best for my skin lotions. I shop at Mary Thē in Maiden Lane." She said this with a laugh as if she were letting down Chinese civilization by shopping on the priciest street in town.

"Anyway I can see that you take good care of yourself." Which was true in a limited way. Anne did watch her diet and neither drank nor smoked. But she thought the nostrums of an herbalist quack and she certainly could not afford to shop in Maiden Lane.

"Some women are not cut out for this," Blossom Wong said slowly, "though I try to make this place as comfortable as I can. I didn't think you were when I first saw you. But you never know. Even I am still learning. Which reminds me Mr. Choong complimented you, my dear. He said, 'She's talented. Very talented.'" Anne could hardly believe her ears. Well, he probably just wanted to cover for himself. And who knew maybe just licking her toes was enough for him though he did ask for reciprocation.

"As for the Qípáo," Blossom Wong said, "why not keep it. It suits you." Of course, it suited her. It was her. The dress she had worn when she met Mr. Okamoto. The dress that made her look and feel classy, like herself not the laundry wife of Geary Quan. Still all kinds of contrary thoughts rushed through Anne's mind. What would her husband say, "Sell it," probably. Or "Think you're Anna May Wong, huh." No, Anne would never let him see her in this dress.

"Thank you very much," Anne said.

"You may call me Auntie Blossom Wong because that is my name. I have grandchildren you know. And a dead husband," she added quickly. Anne was surprised though she didn't show it.

"Yes, I have had quite a life," Blossom Wong said.

Anne could well imagine that.

"Now dear, I have to finish my breakfast."

Blossom Wong stood up. Anne rose almost in unison. Anne bowed slightly as she shook Blossom Wong's hand.

"Oh, here you almost forgot your Qípáo and your shoes," Blossom Wong said with a twinkle in her eye. Anne grabbed the plastic bag into which Blossom Wong had put the Qípáo and her shoes then stepped out into Quincy Alley.

Anne took the Geary Street bus to Japan Town. She stopped briefly in front of the Katsura Garden Bonsai Shop wishing that she had a bonsai in the living room. No, it would be out of place, and it definitely wouldn't suit Geary. As she stepped inside the Japan Center Building, she had no idea where she was going. An older couple passed her speaking in Japanese. Anne was delighted. The language of Mr. Okamoto, how wonderful and exotic it sounded.

Anne climbed the stairs. She went inside the Kinokuniya Bookstore. She was surprised to see so many Japanese fashion magazines. She thumbed through several of them. A man like Mr. Okamoto must have plenty of available women. Was this the competition? Why shouldn't she too have her place? She could tell by the way Mr. Okamoto looked at her that he was quite taken. She had felt like a different woman in the Qípáo. More confident. Or was this due to the fact of being away from her husband? Around him she felt dowdy, and, yes, sexless. Anne picked up a book on Japanese Zen Gardens. She loved the simplicity of the lines and the form. So much less ornate than she was used to. And did this not also say something about sex? She was not, however, sure what it was or if a rock garden should lead to these thoughts.

Anne walked toward the counter. There were several people in front of her. Each person was buying a book or a magazine. Anne felt foolish standing in line with nothing in her hand. Anne herself wasn't quite sure why she did it, but she stepped out of line and walked out of the bookstore. She stood there for a minute. She wanted a translation of Mr. Okamoto's business card. Didn't she? Why not go back in?

Anne watched two Japanese women drinking tea at one of the tables outside the Tan Tan Cafe next to the bookstore. Tea relaxed her. Anne stepped inside. A young Japanese woman was slicing a piece of cake for a customer. Shortly she took Anne's order.

"Tea," Anne said.

The woman looked at Anne as if she expected her to order more.

"Tea," Anne repeated.

As Anne was paying for the tea she thought, *I may as well try. Who knows.*

"Here," Anne said paying for the tea and leaving a five-dollar tip. If the woman was surprised, she showed no sign of it. Anne showed her Mr. Okamoto's business card. "Perhaps you can write this out for me in English." The woman wrote out the translation on the back of an old receipt. Anne took it and the tea from the counter and sat down at the table. With trembling hands, she took several sips of the tea before beginning to read:

Yoshi Okamoto, President and Owner of Okamoto Electronics. There followed the firm's address and phone number in Tokyo.

"Yoshi. Yoshi," Anne kept repeating to herself. She certainly did not want to be sucking his penis and saying in between breaths, "Mr. Okamoto. How wonderful." She wanted to know his first name and to say "Yoshi," even between breaths. What was she thinking? She never thought this way before. No, this was a good sign. But what if this was an outdated business card or the bakery girl had made a mistake? Oh well. She may as well try to contact him. She knew how to keep her secret. She would rent a post office box. Her transfer was still good; she would continue out of Geary Street. She did not want to be seen in the Chinatown Post Office.

***

Anne waited impatiently in line at the New Chinatown Post Office at Geary and Parker Streets. Everyone seemed to need a passport or to mail a package with a lot of customs forms to fill out. An older man shouted at the clerk in almost incomprehensible Mandarin. The man bought just two stamps. He grabbed the change from the postal clerk's hand. He was still shouting as he walked out the door. Another customer stepped up to the postal service counter. She like almost everyone else spoke to postal clerk in Cantonese.

It was now Anne's turn.

"I want a postal box, please."

The other customers in line waited impatiently as Anne filled out the forms and searched her purse for proper identification and an envelope with her address on it. Fortunately, she had an old PG&E utility bill. Finally she got the key. Anne paid and was about to leave when she realized that she needed an envelope with enough air mail postage for Japan.

"Perhaps you can also sell me a piece of paper," Anne said. The clerk looked at Anne exasperated. "The United States Post Office," he said authoritatively, "does not sell paper. You can have this though," he said, giving her a piece of notebook paper then taking her money.

"Some people," Anne heard the woman behind her say. "Some people are just disorganized." Anne paid no attention. She walked to one of the tables alongside the wall and wrote to Yoshi.

9

Yoshi hardly noticed when his secretary put the mail in the mahogany tray on his desk.

"Miss Sakimoto, please phone Dr. Hans Schoeb at Siemens in Berlin. Tell him... No, here, maybe I better write it down." Yoshi wrote on the office stationery.

"The line is busy as usual, Mr. Okamoto," his secretary said. "I'll have to keep trying."

Yoshi leaned back in his chair and surveyed the Tokyo skyline. "Out of the ashes," he mused to himself, "and damn proud of it." He turned back around only to find that his secretary was still trying to get through to Berlin. He thumbed through his mail. On top was a letter to him from San Francisco. The sender's name in the left-hand corner was written in Chinese characters with a post office box address below. Odd that the name wouldn't be written in English; and besides he couldn't remember having dealt with any Chinese businessmen in San Francisco. His curiosity piqued, Yoshi opened the letter. He was surprised to find it written entirely in Chinese characters.

Yoshi's secretary had finally gotten through to Dr. Schoeb. He decided to listen in. He could hear Dr. Schoeb talking in German, a language that sent tingles down his spine. He had come to like dealing with German businessmen. They were punctual and courteous with almost courtly manners. So unlike the Thais or Chinese who always seemed to have something up their sleeves.

His secretary talked in a very even tone of voice. Though he did not understand German, he knew that they did not talk so flat. His secretary held her hand over the receiver and turned toward him. "Anything to add sir?" Yoshi waved his hand. He now spoke into the phone and said his goodbye in very polite Japanese. It was a touch that he had thought of himself, and the Germans loved it.

"Well," Yoshi said impatiently.

"Do you remember Hurricane Blanc?" his secretary responded.

"Yes, certainly," Yoshi replied.

He had heard about it on T.V. Hurricane Blanc had slammed into the East Coast of the United States. It had done its heaviest damage on the coast of Maine. Though several coastal cities in other states suffered heavy damage whole forests near the coast were almost flattened. After he and his wife had watched it on T.V. he was surprised when a few days later he read in the newspaper that only 152 people had died.

"Dr. Schoeb said that the Die Schone Gretl lost 90 containers in that storm. Among them all of ours," Miss Sakimoto said, coming quickly to the point. Yoshi's jaw dropped. He was not surprised that 90 containers had been lost in the storm. No what he was surprised about was that his firm's containers had been stowed on deck. Didn't he have a standing order that all of the Okamoto Electronics Company containers shipped by Hansa Shipping Lines or any other shipping company were to be stowed under deck? No wonder the money hadn't arrived. The company would have to sort it out with the shipping insurer who would get back to the shipping planners at Hansa Shipping Lines.

"Read this for me please. Hopefully it isn't more bad news," Yoshi said, handing his secretary the letter.

"My Chinese isn't too good, sir. But I'll try."

Yoshi smiled. His secretary was a polyglot and that was one of the reasons he had hired her. An almost traditional Japanese woman except in the way she dressed, typically she always understated her abilities. His secretary began:

Dear Mr. Okamoto,

I very much enjoyed meeting you and also our discussion in the lobby of the Hotel Kabuki. I hope to see you again. Write please.

Mr. Quan

"Here, you may want to note the business address and phone number at the top," his secretary said. "It says: The Quan Shang Company, Chinatown, 12 Stark Alley, San Francisco, California 94109.However a postscript says that all correspondence should be sent to the post office box on the envelope."

Yoshi sat there bewildered. He could not recall meeting any Chinese businessmen and certainly none in an alley in Chinatown. All of his business contacts had been in Silicon Valley. The only Chinese he had met in San Francisco was that beautiful Chinese woman. Suddenly it dawned on him. She had written the letter and had written it in such a way as to disguise herself just in case someone other than Yoshi himself read it which was all too likely in an office. He wondered: How she had gotten his address? He had taken a few business cards printed in Japanese. The ones printed in English had been left in his small suitcase with his valuables which, as was his habit, he had locked and put under the bed. Well, what did it matter how she did it? She had written him. Now he knew how to contact her again. He was absolutely delighted.

"Yes," Yoshi said stiffly after quickly composing himself. "I'll contact Mr. Quan next time I'm in San Francisco." And with that he put the letter in the mahogany tray on his desk.

"Mr. Quan," his secretary mused to herself as she stepped away. It was obvious the characters had been written by a woman. In any case, she would keep silent.

10

The house felt cold and empty. How it contrasted with Yoshi's warmth and her response to it. Anne held tightly onto the Qípáo though there was no danger it would slip from her hands. Various hiding places raced through her mind. Under the bed? No. Under the mattress? He would hardly find it there, but what would it do to the Qípáo? Put it in the laundry on a hanger with other clothes hanging around it? That seemed like a good idea, but he sometimes checked through the laundry to make sure customers hadn't left their clothes too long. If they had, he put them up for sale or gave them to the Goodwill. No, again. What about that old flour drawer in the kitchen? They never used it. She could remove the drawer, place the folded Qípáo in two plastic bags just to make sure it gathered no dust, then place a newspaper flat over the plastic bags. They had newspaper on top of the bottom drawers anyway so that if by chance Geary did pull out this drawer, he would not notice the difference. Anne acted quickly. She did as she thought.

Soon afterwards, Anne heard the familiar sound of her husband's 1962 Chevrolet pickup as he parked in Stark Alley. She did not expect him to have a Lincoln Town Car like Yoshi, but certainly they could afford a better car. She was embarrassed to be seen next to him in his old truck. Anne recalled the smell of the leather and sinking into the soft seats of the town car. Now that was sexy.

The bathroom door slammed shut. As usual Geary had not even bothered to say, "Hello." He was always complaining about the water bill, yet every night after work, he filled the tub with water instead of taking a shower. There, she could hear the water running out of the faucet. Well, she may as well make supper. She had just started to wash the bok choy when she heard him bellow. "Anne. Anne." What an ugly voice he had. Anne dried her hands and walked slowly toward the bathroom. Geary sat in the tub, staring straight ahead. "Well?" Anne asked.

"You wash my back. Here is the wash rag. Here is the soap."

Anne dipped the soap in the water, then rubbed it all over his back. She felt his two large moles as her fingers slid over his skin. *In this day and age why doesn't he have them removed?* she thought. *This is not nineteenth century China.* She flattened the wash rag and started scrubbing his back, starting at the spots where the two moles were as if she could wash them away. She moved over to his right shoulder. "Higher," he said. "Harder." Anne winced. What century in China did he think he was in? She rubbed harder. She rubbed higher. He seemed to relax.

"You go back to Blossom Wong's tonight," he said with an angry roll of authority in his voice.

"No," she responded, trying to say it as soothingly as possible.

"No? That's what you said."

"Yes."

"We'll see. We'll see."

Didn't he ever speak in nice full sentences, she thought. Suddenly he stood up.

"Suck penis. Suck penis," he shouted.

It wasn't even hard. And she was supposed to accommodate him? As she started to leave the room, suddenly he slapped her face. Anne was completely stunned. She had never been hit before. Not by her mother. Not by her father. Not by her grandparents. Not even by her husband until now. Anne dropped the soap and wash rag and ran crying from the bathroom.

She flung herself on their bed and continued crying. How long she lay there she could not remember, but suddenly she stopped crying and sat on the edge of the bed. She could go back to China for she was not going to endure this again, for she was sure that this was just the beginning. Or... or what about that phone number the chauffeur had given her?

Where was her husband? She could hear him in the kitchen. Although Anne could have taken the phone number from her purse, she had a good memory for numbers mainly by making up a little formula for them in her head. Her father had taught her this. She held a pillow over the receiver and dialed. "Yes," a voice answered icily. Anne quickly explained, put the receiver down, then she walked into the laundry.

11

Mrs. Huang stood on tiptoes to look into the top loader. She poked with her fingers. She pulled out a faded plaid shirt, smelled it, then started pulling out the rest of the clothes and putting them into the laundry cart. Mrs. Huang hurriedly pushed the cart to a dryer that had a few minutes on the display. As soon as the dryer stopped spinning, she immediately pulled the clothes out and put them in an empty cart. She now piled her clothes into the dryer then quickly put in the coins. An older man with a slight limp and white hair walked up to the dryer. He started to open it. Mrs. Huang grabbed his hand. "Mine now. Mine now," she repeated in Cantonese. "Yours are here," Mrs. Huang said, pointing to the laundry cart near her.

The man felt his clothes, "Not dry," he said angrily.

"Too late," Mrs. Huang said. "Use the other dryer." The man pushed the cart to the next dryer with a resigned look on his face. Mrs. Huang sat smugly in front of the dryer. She had gotten a dryer that was warmed up, and for her that was a triumph.

Anne was surprised that someone would be that pushy to get a warm dryer. For her own part she was enjoying folding the clothes for the wash and fold service they had. She had gotten into a rhythm as she folded each one in a certain way over and over again. At nine-thirty her husband came in to help clean up and to count the money. *I guess the chauffeur isn't coming after all,* Anne thought. Maybe she shouldn't have phoned him in the first place. She continued folding clothes, wishing the night were over and it was another day.

"Fire Inspection. Fire Inspection," someone yelled in loud Cantonese. Anne looked up. It was the chauffeur. Fire inspection? What was going on?

"I will talk with the owners about the inspection. Everyone else, out. Out."

A slightly stooped woman in faded black trousers stood defiantly by her dryer.

"All clear in fifteen minutes," the chauffeur said now realizing that it would be very difficult even for him to get the customers to leave if they did not think they could return for their clothes.

"All clear in fifteen minutes," the chauffeur repeated. The old woman in faded black trousers left. The other customers filed out behind her.

Geary walked briskly up to the chauffeur.

"Where is your identification?" he demanded.

"You will see it soon enough."

"I want to see it now."

"Is that your wife?" the chauffeur asked.

"Yes, yes. What business is it of yours?"

"She has a black eye."

"Well, what of it? I gave it to her."

"A man should never beat his wife."

"Why not? What business is it of yours? Out. Out. You are an impostor."

"No, your wife must leave. Go ma'am. Go out with the others."

Anne ran out of the door. What was the chauffeur going to do? Her heart raced beneath her breast.

"Out," Geary shouted. "You are not a fire inspector. You are an impostor."

"You wanted to see my badge?" the chauffeur asked sarcastically.

"Yes. Where the hell is it?"

The chauffeur rolled up his sleeve. Geary stood there transfixed. He knew immediately that it was the tattoo of one of the Chinese gangs. At that instant the chauffeur kneed him in the balls. Then as he was falling down, he kneed him in the chin. Geary was sprawled out on the floor only the chauffeur wasn't through with him. He grabbed his hair and pulled him up, then shoved a Colt .45 in his face. He shouted at Geary. "It is an honor to be married to a Chinese woman, especially one from the People's Republic of China. You will never hit or mistreat your wife in any way again. Understand. Speak up."

"Yes. Yes," Geary answered as loudly as he could.

"If you ever beat your wife again... and I will know..." the chauffeur pressed the barrel of the 45 against Geary's temple, "the next time you will meet your ancestors."

The chauffeur pushed Geary to the floor, kicked him in the stomach, and slowly walked out the door.

"Fire inspection over. Fire inspection over," the chauffeur shouted almost laughing. The customers looked at one another. Mrs. Huang pushed her way forward and walked through the door. The other customers hesitated a second, then filed in behind her.

Mrs. Huang almost stumbled over Geary as she went to fold her clothes. The other customers acted as if they had never even seen Geary. Except for Mr. Choi. "I go phone police," he said starting out the door.

Mrs. Huang grabbed him by the arm. "What are you, crazy. Gang. Gang trouble. Shut your mouth. You'll live longer. And so will I," she added. Mr. Choi stopped dead in his tracks. He walked back to his dryer without saying a word.

Anne bent over her husband. She didn't know whether he was seriously hurt or even going to recover. She was sure that the chauffeur could have killed him if he wished. She actually felt sorry for her husband. She put her hand to his forehead. She held her hand against his chest, feeling it expand and contract, but very slowly. She did not have the strength to lift her husband and no customer offered to help her.

Anne decided to stay by her husband until he became conscious. Though she did not like to admit it to herself, a part of her wished he would die. Then she would be free for Yoshi and to make love with him as she wished. If only he would respond to her letter, she thought. Twenty minutes went by. It was ten o'clock. Closing time. But because of the chauffeur's "fire inspection" some of the customers had not finished. Mrs. Huang glared at them as if to say: Hurry up or you're dead. Shortly they all left with their bundles and laundry baskets. Mrs. Huang left right on the heels of Mr. Choi, almost pushing him out the door.

For a moment Anne thought of killing Geary though how she would do it she did not know. Gradually he began to move. First stretching his legs, then slowly rolling over on his stomach, then pushing himself up. Anne put her arm around Geary and helped him into the apartment and tucked him in the bed.

Anne went into the kitchen to make a cup of tea. She brought the tea from the counter and sat down at the table. With trembling hands, she took several sips of the tea before beginning to cry.

She lay down on the couch and in her heart wished that Geary would not wake up in the morning.

12

When Anne went into the bathroom that morning she could see blood in the toilet bowl. She was about to flush it, but then, silly as it seemed, she thought she would urinate into Geary's blood, and that his blood and her urine would mix, then be flushed down the toilet.

Anne looked for traces of blood on the floor as she walked into the bedroom, but she found none. His bleeding was internal then, she told herself. Geary was lying in bed face up. She put her hand on his forehead. It was warm, but not hot. He opened his eyes. She smiled in spite of herself.

"Phone Yuan at the repair shop for me," he said quietly. "I'll tell you the phone number."

"Geary sick?" Yuan said. "That's a new one. It must be serious."

"We don't know yet. It may be a day or two," Anne replied.

"Well, don't worry. Tell him he's still on the payroll."

Anne hung up the phone and told Geary. He smiled. Although he knew he was a good mechanic, it was nice to be appreciated by his boss.

Anne went into the kitchen and got a large glass of orange juice. She carefully carried it back into the bedroom. "I'll help you sit up Geary," she said as she put the orange juice on the bedside table. Geary pulled his head up slightly. She eased his pillow up, and moved the one over from her side, placing both against the headboard.

"Here we go," Anne said. She put both hands underneath his armpits and pulled up while Geary sat up and pushed back. She was disappointed in herself, for he had done almost all the work himself.

Geary started to reach for the glass of orange juice. "I'll get it," Anne said as she handed it to him. He drank slowly, cautiously. When he was finished, he held the glass in his lap and stared straight ahead. She took the glass from his hand, went into the bathroom, brought out a wash rag, and wiped the edges of his mouth.

"My breakfast," Geary said in an almost inaudible tone of voice.

"Bacon and eggs wouldn't be so good today," Anne replied. "Perhaps a little wonton soup." Geary shook his head and smiled. He kept staring straight ahead.

There are various kinds of wonton soup. Most of them Anne thought would be too thick and heavy for Geary.

The old butcher block next to the kitchen sink had seen better days. Meat had been hacked on it and the wood had been worn by scrubbings so many times that it had a surface as contorted as a Chinese demon mask. What butcher shop had it come from? Anne had often wondered.

Anne took a meat cleaver from the knife rack. She chopped up the green onions. Soon she was stirring them into the soup. Most of their kitchen utensils were simple and plain, like the U.S. Navy knives, forks, and spoons. Anne looked for a soup bowl that was at least cheerful. The best she could find was a bowl that was a very light blue. She poured the soup from the pot through a strainer and into the bowl.

A broad smile crossed Geary's face, almost like a little boy's, when Anne brought in the soup. As he took the bowl from her hands, his movements seemed much more sure than when she had brought him the orange juice. Geary drank the soup slowly, pausing now and then, obviously enjoying himself.

"Geary, I have to open the laundry now," Anne said.

"No, wait. In the medicine cabinet, there's some tiger balm. Rub a little on my chest."

On his chest? Anne thought as she reached for the jar. When she had looked through the laundry window she had seen the chauffeur knee him in the balls. No, he would not want tiger balm on them. Anne pulled up Geary's T-shirt and gently rubbed on the tiger balm. Certainly, it would do no harm, and perhaps it distracted him from the pain. Then, too, he may have wanted to feel her touch. Anne screwed the top back on and put it on the table next to the lamp.

"Geary, I'll be in the laundry." Anne knew that he wanted her to kiss him, but she could not bring herself to do it. She had not forgotten.

13

Monica and her little sister Lisa ran from one end of the laundry to the other, back and forth. Anne had never seen such rosy-cheeked little girls. She wondered what part of China their family had come from. Their mother Tammy had just taken the clothes out of the dryer and was folding them, completely indifferent to her daughters' noise and giggles.

Just then, as if on cue, Mrs. Sheh walked in carrying her clothes in her Gump's shopping bag and walking with a stiff majestic gait, as if she were about to be ushered in to see the Empress dowager. Little Lisa ran right into her leg. Mrs. Sheh continued toward the counter, though now with a slight hobble, her face bearing an imperious scowl. She put the Gump's bag on the counter and let out a long sigh.

"In my day," she began, in Mandarin. "Oh, I almost forgot you people do not speak proper Mandarin. In my day," she began again in Cantonese, "children were well behaved. And as for little girls they were always quiet and showed respect for their elders." This speech had no effect whatsoever on the running, giggling girls though they now definitely avoided Mrs. Sheh.

There were several customers in the back. One woman was bent over the wash basin apparently wringing out some socks. Suddenly the woman whirled around, and Anne recognized Mrs. Teng. *Oh no*, Anne thought.

"In your day," Mrs. Teng said in shrill Cantonese that even Anne found alarming, "in your day little girls at ten years old, even younger, were sold into prostitution. Babies were left abandoned. Though none of these things happened to ladies of your class."

The two little girls had stopped playing and were now huddled around their mother. Mrs. Sheh put her finger to her lips. "The children," she said, imploring.

"The children can learn history right here. In this laundry. And at least it will be the truth. I am glad Chairman Mao ended your day. Landlords squeezing every cent from the peasants, men carrying the likes of you in a palinquin and being treated like pack animals. Your day is finished, and I am glad of it."

"In my day," Mrs. Sheh replied as if she had not heard a thing, "we had the Peking opera and fabulous nightclubs. In my day, we had civilization."

Mrs. Sheh now turned on her heel and with a very stately gait, walked toward the door.

A silence descended on the Quan Shang Laundry. Finally, one older man spoke up.

"Communist?" he asked.

"No," Mrs. Teng replied emphatically, "retired sewing woman who is over-sexed." The man turned away from Mrs. Teng and quickly began stuffing his clothes in the washer.

14

Three days later, Geary went back to work. He was different now. A little more reserved, a little less aggressive. But these changes were subtle and not enough for Anne. And, after a while, when they could have sex again, she still had no feeling for him, nor did he seem to care.

One evening, about an hour before closing, Geary was fixing one of the washers and Anne was folding clothes for their wash and fold service when the phone rang. Anne stepped over to the counter to answer it. She was surprised to hear Blossom Wong's voice. "My dear, I am a little short of girls this evening," she said apologetically. "Perhaps you can help me out. But, if you don't want to, I truly understand." Anne was speechless for a moment. She had not expected to ever hear from Blossom Wong again.

"There are plenty of other girls in Chinatown," Anne replied.

"Yes, but there aren't that many with class. And besides, you're well liked here." Anne could hardly understand this. She thought the other girls detested her. Well, maybe they didn't.

Hearing no answer, Blossom Wong took this for a no. "I'm quite sorry to have bothered you dear. I understand."

"No, wait," Anne said. She wanted to come and go as she pleased. If she said yes, it would provide a perfect excuse. "Yes, I'll come if you need me."

"Don't hurry, but come as soon as you can, you needn't bring your Qípáo."

Anne waited until Geary had finished repairing the washing machine. He walked over to the counter with his toolbox. Anne motioned him behind the counter and then to the space where they had racks of clothes further back. "Geary," Anne began hesitantly. "Blossom Wong wants me to work this evening. And maybe other times," she added, lying.

Geary shrugged his shoulders, "Go ahead," he said indifferently.

15

The bouncer's unflinching eye stared out at Anne through the peephole. Anne stood in Quincy Alley cold and wondering why the door didn't immediately spring open. She was just about to pound on the door in frustration when it swung open as if blown by a strong gust of wind.

Even though it was her second time there, Anne was once again startled by the contrast with the bleakness of the alley and the opulence of the parlor. There were several antique hanging scrolls that she had not noticed before that had elegant calligraphy and there were the silk tapestries of beautiful scenes of mountains and waterfalls. The Persian rug seemed thicker and more colorful than before. She looked over the intricately carved chairs with dragon's heads at the ends of the armrests. They seemed even more exquisitely carved than she had first noticed.

She was, however, surprised to see two beautiful women in elegant Qípáos sitting in two of them. Blossom Wong stepped out of her room, and as always, she appeared as if she were about to preside over a party in Shanghai to which only ambassadors, top military men, favored artists, and well-heeled financiers were invited.

Blossom Wong extended both hands. Anne did likewise. Blossom Wong held Anne's hands for a moment, the whole time scrutinizing her from head to toe. "Yes, yes dear I certainly appreciate this favor." Seeing Anne eyeing the two women seated in the parlor, Blossom Wong said, "My dear, I always have two of my girls in here. As for you, you're needed in room four." At this Anne winced. "Don't worry. It isn't that sort of thing." Blossom Wong laughed.

"You know, I've thought about it," Anne said, biting her lower lip slightly. "Perhaps I could work here from time to time."

"Well, then, I was wrong about you," Blossom Wong said. "See even I have something to learn. Now you know where the shower is." Blossom Wong turned around slowly and returned to her room.

As soon as Anne had finished her shower and dressed in one of the Qípáos hanging in the bathroom, she walked toward room four. Apprehensively, she opened the door. There were three gorgeous women in Qípáos seated on a raised futon. Musical instruments were next to them.

"Well here finally," one of them said. "We were wondering when you were going to come."

Anne blushed. She was glad she had taken a quick shower.

"Do you know how to play the Húgín?" one of them with very high cheekbones asked.

Anne shook her head

"Can you play the Yuèqín?"

Anne shook her head again.

"And the xiäo?"

"No, I studied classical music. I play the piano," Anne said.

"That won't help much here," one of them said giggling. The other two put their hands to their mouths.

"We play these instruments. Not quite like in a Chinese opera, but we have practiced together."

Anne started to get up. If she could not play an instrument, then she may as well leave.

"Oh, don't leave. You will play something too."

Anne looked around the room. What other instrument was there to play? There certainly was no piano.

"You will play the flute."

"But I told you."

"You know how to play this flute."

"The xiäo?" Anne asked.

"No, no. If you cannot play an instrument, then you are the go-down girl," one of them said, laughing.

"The what?"

"You go down on the man's penis and keep in harmony with our playing. Think you can do that?"

"Now get undressed."

"Am I the only one?"

"We are the orchestra. We don't get undressed. But afterward, you may put on the Pèi behind you."

Anne looked behind her. On a hanger was one of the most beautiful Pèis she had ever seen. It was made of light-yellow silk thread and had beautifully embroidered red dragons. Each side of the collar was surrounded by a black lattice design. It was so simple yet so elegant. One of the girls took it off the hanger and handed it to Anne. She ran her hands lightly over the silk and put it to her cheek. She had only seen something like this in a history book.

"Let me comb your hair," one of the girls said. Her friend held out her hand and took the Pèi from Anne.

Now what is this about? Anne asked herself. The women gently brushed out Anne's hair in long sweeping strokes until it hung freely about her shoulders. She did this almost as if she was a hairdresser and perhaps she was one, for the women working here had other jobs.

"Now, get undressed," the women said.

Anne hesitated; she did not like to get undressed in front of other women. But at the thought of putting on the Pèi, she readily began to take off her clothes. The three women stood back looking at her body. They had never seen such taut breasts and shapely legs. Anne felt their eyes and their approval.

"Now here is your Pèi," one of them said as she stepped up behind Anne and helped Anne slip into it. How wonderful it felt against her skin. It was everything she had imagined and then some. It caressed her breasts like a man's hands. She stepped over to the mirror and looked at herself. She reached behind her feeling for a sash or something to tie the front together. There was none. But the split down the front, like her very inner self, with her pubic hair showing quite vividly, that look seemed to go with the Pèi.

"Let me explain your role," the woman with the very high cheekbones said. She began to tell Anne what to do while the others held their hands over their mouths giggling like little schoolgirls.

"Well, now, shall we begin? The man is waiting." Each of them picked up her instrument. They filed out the door and went down the hallway. Anne followed. They stopped. One of them eased open a door, then quietly as cats, they entered the room.

Anne was surprised to see the room was only illuminated by one large flickering candle, which was on a table in front of a statue of the Buddha. She could see a

Chinese man lying face up on a low bed, covered up to his neck with a comforter. One of the women pulled the comforter slowly off him. Anne was happy to see that he was quite muscular. But if he could afford to come here, he certainly could afford to go to a gym. A slight smile crossed the man's face. Each of the three musicians seated herself on a cushion, and Anne sat on the cushion next to the bed. The woman playing the Xiäo began slowly, then the Húgín, and the Yuèqín chimed in.

Anne was so taken by the charm of the music that she knelt there transfixed. A tap on her shoulder reminded her of her part. Anne bent over the man until her hair just touched his chest. Then, in harmony with the music, Anne moved her head so that her hair tickled the man's face, then his chest, then his stomach. The music now stopped, and Anne stopped with it. She raised her head slightly, her hair no longer on the man. The music began again only this time, starting with the strumming of the Húgín next the Yuèqín, then the Xiäo. The beat was now faster. The music slightly higher pitched. Anne lowered her head again, her hair brushed against the man's face, then his chest and navel. The music slowed and Anne's hair brushed lightly against the man's erect penis then his testicles. There was a pause, and then Anne began again. With the sound of the Xiäo she now circled his penis and testicles with her hair, brushing them lightly.

Anne now lowered herself slightly and began caressing him in exactly the same manner with her breasts. Keeping in time with the music. Then there was a pause. Anne clamped her teeth gently on the head of his penis and enfolded it with her lips.

The woman who had been playing the Xiäo now sang a song in high falsetto from the Chinese opera. "The Lady with a Red- Marked Hand." The Húgín was strummed while Anne moved her head in time with the music. Just as she could feel the man's penis began to well up with semen, the music and the singing stopped. Anne paused. The music and singing continued with a faster beat. Stopped. Then continued even faster. Anne followed with her head in rhythm. She could now taste his semen hot in her mouth. The Húgín and the Yuèqín concluded quickly. The woman who played the Xiäo now played a tune that slowly wound down.

Anne looked at the man. The whole time he had acted as if he were in a dream. Now he seemed to be dreaming in a higher state of consciousness.

Anne got up slowly and went back to room four to rinse out her mouth. Someone had laid out a toothbrush and toothpaste on the side of the sink. Anne rinsed and brushed more as a matter of hygiene than any concern about having the man's semen in her mouth. Actually, she found it quiet pleasant.

Shortly, the three women came in and the man was now alone with the flickering candle, his dreams, and the Buddha. The woman who had played the Yuèqín placed several hundred-dollar bills on the small table with the lamp. "Take three hundred," she said. "And don't worry about Blossom Wong. She's been well taken care of."

"You were quite good you know," the woman who played the Xiäo said.

"I was only following you as best I could," Anne replied.

"No, no, we were following you."

Was this true? Anne thought. Was she that sexually talented? It did seem to her that she was following them. But could they have been following her? Could they? Anne thought about it. Perhaps this was her true Buddha nature.

16

There were days when Anne was overwhelmed. Today was a day like that. Anne had no sooner opened the door of the laundry than seven customers pushed their laundry carts in the door. Each of them ran to their favorite washer. One woman who was quite stocky began taking another woman's laundry out of the washer just as fast as the other woman could put it in. "This is mine. This is mine," the stocky woman repeated. Finally the second woman, perhaps because she was a little thinner or was just intimidated, gave in.

"Army wife, huh. You always get your way."

"My husband fought in Korea. Maybe you should show some respect."

"Your husband is old. You are very frustrated."

Angry, the woman now took her clothes and went to a washer in the next aisle.

Four more customers dropped wash and fold laundry off. Anne had still not caught up with the laundry from yesterday. And now since so many washers were being used Anne had to scatter the clothes in different washers in the laundry. It was very hard keeping track and sometimes Anne made mistakes.

A man wearing a faded brown business suit with a thin scar above his right eye entered the laundry. He walked up to the counter and gave his name.

"Wah Fung Yim. My laundry." Anne searched for several minutes, looking through the plastic bags of clothes with the tags written in Chinese characters. Finally when she was about to give up she found it underneath the counter. "Here," Anne said, putting the bag on the counter. "Six dollars." The man opened the plastic bag and began to look through the clothes, even pulling out some of them.

"Four black socks are missing. Four black socks are missing," he shouted. Anne walked back to the shelf where they put lost and found clothes. There were no black socks.

"I am Wah Fung Yim. I will see a lawyer." He threw down six dollars, grabbed the bag and stormed out the door. Anne turned away from the front of the counter.

She started crying softly to herself. How could she tell her husband? How stupid of her to lose the socks.

As Anne was wiping away her tears Mrs. Teng entered, pushing a laundry cart overflowing with laundry.

"So much wash Mrs. Teng and so many times a week," Anne exclaimed now feeling a little better.

"I wash for the people in the apartment house. It's a little money and it keeps me busy when I'm not having sex."

"Mrs. Teng," Anne implored.

Mrs. Teng found a couple of washers in the back of the laundry. Anne breathed a sigh of relief. Although she liked Mrs. Teng she found her overwhelming, and Anne certainly did not want her to talk about the suck-suck girl. After all what had she been doing in Blossom Wong's just a couple of weeks ago, and no doubt again soon. A silence descended on the Quan Shang Laundry. It was all too brief.

Mrs. Teng had just finished a load of clothes and was about to put them in one of the few empty dryers available when a man next to her with thinning gray hair started to do the same.

"You should let me go first," Mrs. Teng said firmly.

"Why should I? We were both here at the same time. We should flip for it."

The man pulled out a quarter from his pocket. "Heads or tails?"

"What?" Mrs. Teng exclaimed. "I am a woman. I should go first. Have you no manners?"

"You are too aggressive to be a woman. Especially a Chinese woman."

Mrs. Teng suddenly hurled her clothes into the dryer and fed in the quarters. "Don't tell me what a Chinese woman should be like."

"You are not like a Chinese woman."

"No? Chinese woman. See." Mrs. Teng pulled up her dress, pulled down her panties revealing surprising shapely thighs and a mass of pubic hair. The man started to turn his head away.

"Put on your glasses. Look," Mrs. Teng shouted. "Chinese woman. Chinese woman. See. You foolish Chinese men you want to gamble for the dryer... for everything. I try other men. White men, Black men, Samoan men,... I know you Chinese men are not as good as you think."

"We Chinese men are the best," the man said proudly.

"Ever try anything else?"

"Why should I?"

"How can you tell which is best if you don't try anything else?"

Anne thought this was true for her at least. A Japanese man, that was who she was in love with.

"No white man would have you," the man said sharply.

"Oh, I had Alex Ivanoff last night."

"He's too young for you."

"No, maybe I'm too hot for him. Besides he has big meat, not like you."

"How do you know?"

"Pull down your pants."

"Bull."

The man put his clothes in a nearby dryer that was just empty. What should he say? What could he say? Anne was impressed that the man stood there proudly as if he represented Chinese civilization itself. But where was his triumph? Mrs. Teng had the dryer and the last word, and he did not.

The day passed more easily in the afternoon. Anne kept dreading Geary's arrival. While she hardly thought Geary would hit her after the beating the chauffeur had given him, he could yell, he could intimidate. He could threaten her.

Anne heard Geary's pickup in the alley. The time had come. Anne walked out to the pickup. Geary looked at her surprised. "Well, what is it?" he said impatiently.

"Mr. Wah Fung Yim is going to sue us. I lost his things," Anne said fearfully.

"Stupid. You should pay more attention. What did you lose?"

"Four black socks."

"Is that all?"

"Yes."

"You definitely are just from China," Geary said.

"Do you know the price of a lawyer in this city?"

Anne shook her head.

"Try $200 an hour, and more. And small claims court. Forget it."

They went into the house together. Anne laughed, cried, then laughed again. Geary kept laughing.

That night for once she felt comfortable with her husband in bed. Sex, while certainly not as good as with Yoshi, was warm and at least she had a climax.

17

Anne had anticipated this day. It had been three weeks since she had written to Yoshi and now here she was in the New Chinatown Post Office standing in front of her mail box. She put the key in the slot, turned, closed her eyes, then opened the door. Anne stood there for a moment maybe more, blinked and her eyes were open. Her heart raced. There was a letter there. She reached for it slowly as if anticipating it was an illusion. She touched it lightly, then gripped it firmly. Anne now tore the letter open. Under the elegant Okamoto Electronics letterhead it read:

Dear Sir,

I was very pleased to receive your letter. Your company product is indeed important to Okamoto Electronics. I trust that your firm will continue to develop and refine it. In the near future when I am in San Francisco my representative will contact you, and we shall continue to discuss this matter.

Cordially,

Mr. Yoshi Okamoto

President of Okamoto Electronics

Anne kissed the letter. "Yoshi. Yoshi." She said it again and again. She put it back in the envelope and into her purse. As she walked outside, she looked up at the sky. It was blue with hardly a cloud.

Anne was hungry. Perhaps she should hurry home and cook herself lunch. No, why not treat herself? Why not enjoy this day? She walked over to Clement Street, the heart of New Chinatown.

The buildings on Clement Street were more squarish than Anne liked. There were no pagodas or steep sloping tiled roofs. But there were the crowds of Chinese shopping at the markets, the bent over old men and women and the mothers with babies strapped to their backs.

There were so many Chinese restaurants it was hard to know which one to choose. But why Chinese? There were a few other restaurants like the one right near where she was standing: Mai's Vietnamese Restaurant.

Anne sat down at a table next to the wall. Above her there was a watercolor painting of a woman carrying a basket with a pineapple and a bunch of bananas. She picked up the menu. There was nothing she was familiar with. Number 31 Ta Pin Lu, Number 32 Bo Nhung. Further... Number 35 Tom Xau Lang, looked interesting. Next to it in English was written: Sautéed prawns with coconut curry sauce.

The waiter brought Anne tea and took her order. The sonorous sounds of Vietnamese filled the air. Against this backdrop the one couple speaking English sounded atonal. The Tom Xau Lang arrived sooner than she expected. Not surprisingly it was sweet yet hot. As Anne ate it, she was glad not to be eating her own cooking for once. Food seemed to taste better when cooked by someone else. After she had finished eating, she sipped her tea, then paid, leaving a dollar tip, wishing it could have been more.

Back out on Clement Street Anne heard the sound of a Chinese opera coming from a speaker somewhere. Although this was quite common in Chinatown, it was the first time she heard it here. She followed her ears and was soon inside the Chung Chou City Herb and Tea Company. She could hardly believe her eyes when she saw the price of shark fins. 179 dollars a pound. *Who would pay that much?* she thought. There were teas and herbs from Burma, Thailand, and China. There were also dried mushrooms. That was it. Geary would like mushrooms and that would certainly explain her trip. After Anne paid she lingered, listening to the music.

Anne continued browsing, finally stopping in front of the Joseph Yan Art Gallery. She looked through the window, admiring the calligraphy and the paintings especially one black brush painting of two cranes, one flying above a pine branch on which another was perched.

It seemed like forever until the 2 Clement bus arrived. In her purse Anne had a letter from Yoshi and a bag of mushrooms for Geary. Soon she would be back in the laundry, but now she had hope.

18

It was several weeks later; Anne was working in the laundry doing her daily routine when the phone rang. Perhaps it was due to the noise in the laundry, but at first Anne did not recognize the chauffeur's voice nor hear him completely. "At seven o'clock this evening." What was this person talking about? He spoke to her again, louder this time, "Mr. Okamoto will see you this evening at seven o'clock. Please be outside at Stockton and Stark Alley." Anne looked up at the clock on the wall, it was 3:45 p.m. There was plenty of time to bathe and get herself ready.

Anne wished she could be with Yoshi. Right now, instantly. She kept looking at the clock. Time had its own pace. Customers came and went until, like it or not, the moment came when she could get ready.

As Anne was about to go out the door and into their apartment, Geary came into the laundry. She motioned him outside. "Blossom Wong's tonight," Anne said briskly. "She gave me a Qípáo to wear." Geary looked at her angrily, and then, without saying a word, stepped back into the laundry. But why was he annoyed? He had after all started this, she told herself.

Shortly, but not as soon as she wished, Anne was wearing her Qípáo and waiting at Stockton and Stark Alley.

As the chauffeur guided the Lincoln Town Car through the night Anne closed her eyes. If only it were possible for Yoshi to be there when she opened them. Time now seemed to speed by like in a dream. They were in the lobby of the Hotel Kabuki, then in the elevator, down the corridor, and finally in front of Yoshi's door.

Anne was barely in the room when she began to take off her Qípáo. Yoshi was certainly partly prepared himself, for he stood in the center of the room in his boxer shorts, bare feet, and T-shirt. He took one long look at Anne, said something in Japanese that sounded like an apology, then stepped into the bathroom.

Anne wanted Yoshi to remember this night, and to want to see her again and again. She wanted a lover. Her husband was not her lover. There was no electricity in his touch. No sweetness in his voice. And when they were finished having sex she lay there and looked at the ceiling while he rolled over and went to sleep. And those anonymous men in Blossom Wong's? While she could not deny that she enjoyed herself with most of them, who were they to her? And, for them, was she not just a plaything?

When Yoshi returned from the bathroom, he still had his underwear on. He was so modest Anne thought. And so precise. Even his shoes next to the bed had the toes perfectly in line, so that one shoe was not even a millimeter ahead or behind the other. Anne, too, had her bra and panties on, but that was for effect. She had decided that the way to win his heart, at least this time, was to take the initiative. She pressed herself against him and whispered into his ear in Cantonese, "You are so handsome." Anne then pushed him away. She now motioned him to bend forward, then pulled off his T-shirt. She smiled, happy to see the rippling muscles of his stomach. Then she quickly pulled down his boxer shorts. She looked at his penis and said "Oh my, big boy," then with an abrupt motion that startled Yoshi, and was much more forceful then he had expected Anne pushed him onto the bed.

Yoshi could see Anne bending over at the foot of the bed. *What next?* he thought. Anne was reaching into her purse where she had a set of small cymbals that she had bought at Yuen Kung's in Chinatown. The cymbals were about four inches in diameter. Anne held the cymbals closely in front of her and, with her back toward Yoshi, walked to the center of the room. Anne paused, then turned around, and beat the cymbals together. She then began singing a song in a high falsetto from the Chinese Opera "The Faithful Concubine."

Yoshi was completely taken aback. He turned toward her on his side, his eyes and ears alert. Anne raised her right knee up, her hands straight up in the air. She banged the cymbals together above her head. Then she turned sideways, straightened her right leg and cocked her left knee in the air while extending her right arm upward, then returned to a standing position, and clanged the cymbals together. She stopped singing and put the cymbals on the floor and gingerly slipped out of her bra and panties.

Anne picked up the cymbals, crossed them in front of her breasts and again began to sing. She cocked her right leg across her left almost concealing her pubic hair, straightened up, walked forward with a coquettish mincing gait, clashed the cymbals together and stamped her feet on the floor.

Yoshi looked at Anne who was now a completely still figure looking at him with piercing demon eyes. He felt a chill go down his spine and wanted to huddle underneath the covers.

Suddenly Anne smiled. Her eyes became soft, and her body animated. Laughing and now speaking in Cantonese she climbed on the bed. She bent over Yoshi, swishing her hair back and forth over his penis and testicles, she stopped a moment, took a nibble almost like a fish, paused, moved her head up and down several times, then stood up, her legs on either side of him. She slowly undulated her hips and lowered herself onto his penis. But as soon as it was just barely inside Anne stopped. It was not for nothing that she worked at Blossom Wong's. Anne now reached down for her cymbals. She banged them together, sang a verse from "The Faithful Concubine" then almost instantly she pressed herself against Yoshi until he had a delicious pain that seemed to extend to his pubic bone. Another clash of the cymbals, this time ringing in Yoshi's ear. Anne now moved up and down singing in a falsetto and clashing the cymbals, so that Yoshi felt that his whole inner being was reverberating. He reached up for Anne's breasts, but she playfully fended off his groping hands with the cymbals. Finally, Yoshi reached them and tickled her nipples as Anne kept thrusting and thrusting.

Yoshi's semen flowed, flowed, and flowed, his head still reverberating from the cymbals. He could feel her long hair as she kissed him. Was he in heaven or here on earth?

Anne shut the door to Yoshi's room. The hotel corridor was empty. As she walked toward the elevator Anne felt like she had left one world and entered another.

The chauffeur was waiting for her in the hotel lobby. He seemed in a jocular mood. "Several people complained about the noise," he said with a smile. "I had to speak with the manager."

"I didn't mean to cause so much trouble," Anne said.

"No, no, I told him you were a Chinese opera singer who needed to practice her singing while playing the cymbals, to make sure her part was just right. From 'The Faithful Concubine' wasn't it miss?"

"Well, yes."

"You weren't bad, but you deviated from the plot."

Anne didn't know if this were due to his knowledge of the opera or if he had made a sharp observation as to what had really happened.

"Are you ready then miss?"

"Certainly."

As they started to walk out the door Anne could see a scowl on the desk clerk's face. And so? Yoshi was upstairs dreaming of her and nothing else could make any difference.

19

Anne awoke in the night. She had a dream that she was in a strange bed with a strange man and that he was fat and bearing on her until she could hardly breathe. She lay there gasping. Had she held her breath in her sleep? Geary lay next to her breathing slowly but deeply. If he were Yoshi, she would press her breasts against him, whisper in his ear, and reach down to feel if his penis were hard.

Perhaps if she thought about something else, she would fall back to sleep. There was a beautiful garden behind her parents' house in Guangzhou. Anne tried to remember it as it was, as she had played in it. She did this, enjoying the scene. Now though instead of being lulled to sleep, she was more awake than ever. There was nothing to do but get up, go in the kitchen and make herself some tea.

Without a meal being cooked, groceries being put away, or even a dinner with Geary, the kitchen seemed cold and barren. Anne cinched the belt of her bathrobe. Sitting there in the dark by herself felt good. Anne was about to get up, turn on the light, and make herself tea when through the window curtains she saw several men walk out of the warehouse across the street. A large truck backed into Stark Alley. Now, Anne told herself, was not the time to turn on the kitchen light. Although she did not know how to identify it, the truck was actually a tractor-trailer with a twenty-foot container on a chassis. One man with bolt cutters cut the seal and lock on the door, then two men struggled to open the container doors. Two other men walked to the entrance of Stark Alley and stationed themselves there. Both of them had their hands in their pockets as if they held weapons. The loading dock doors of the warehouse now swung open. Anne looked at a scene like a gangster movie, a fat Chinese man, puffing on a cigar, began to bark orders. Two men climbed into the container and started to push and slide crates toward the doors. Four men, two on each side, carried these crates the short distance to the loading dock. From the way the men strained and cursed it was obvious the crates were quite heavy. What did they contain? Anne wondered. The only thing she could think of was rifles, or guns of some sort, and ammunition. Perhaps drugs could also be in the crates. Inside the warehouse other men with dollies moved and stacked the crates. Almost before Anne knew it the warehouse doors were shut, the container closed, and the tractor-trailer driven away. The side door of the warehouse now opened and the boss and his men filed out. They stood there in Stark Alley, some of them smoking cigarettes. A sedan backed into Stark Alley and about half the men got in. Then shortly another sedan backed in, doors slammed, the sedans drove away, and Stark Alley was quiet again.

Except for the swearing and the slamming of the doors at the end, Anne was surprised at how noiseless and quick the operation had been. She thought about telling Geary, but undoubtedly, he knew. She decided that she like him would remain silent.

20

Anne pretended not to notice when Alex Ivanoff entered the Quan Shang Laundry. He seemed to be in a foul mood as he rolled his seabag off his shoulder and into the laundry basket. As usual he pulled out a twenty-dollar bill. He snapped it down on the counter.

"I heard about Mrs. Teng," Alex said in a whiskey voice.

"Well she often just says things," Anne replied looking up at Alex who at six foot four towered above her.

"Exactly what?"

Anne remained silent. She did not want to reply, especially in front of the customers... though what was the use, the Quan Shang Laundry held no secrets.

"Bragged about going down on me. Did she?"

"No," Anne replied. "Anyway nobody believed her. Besides she's older than you."

"But it's true."

Anne lowered her voice. "Like I said, she didn't say anything about going down on you."

"Well she did. And about her being older, don't think she isn't hot."

Though Anne said nothing she was taken aback. She had thought Mrs. Teng may have been kidding about Alex Ivanoff.

"First Dominic fires me from the coffee gang because I'm drunk and won't give him the rest of my whiskey. Then somehow I end up in the Club Hong Kong where I hooked up with Mrs. Teng."

"I've heard of it," Anne said. Just about everyone in Chinatown had heard of it. A low-class cellar bar near Stockton and Pacific. It was a hangout for Chinese gangsters and anyone who wanted to spend money. There was gambling in the back and women for sale for a drink and the right price. Her husband drank there sometimes. She wondered if some of the money she gave him didn't go to them.

"I hope you got out of there all right," Anne said.

"We got out all right. I had my arm around her waist as she led me over to her apartment. She felt hot even before we hit the door. Just as we step inside, she goes down on me then she had her dress off and we were making it on the floor. No panties. A woman of her age and no panties."

Mrs. Teng, Anne thought, now held no surprises and no secrets.

"Most Chinese woman aren't like that," Anne said a bit hastily.

"Maybe, but you've got class. Anyone can see that. You're definitely no Mrs. Teng."

Anne wished she were sometimes. Then she would have stood up to her husband more. No, what difference would it have made? Yoshi was her lover. Now Yoshi was the man in her life.

21

The Qípáo along with several others Blossom Wong had loaned her, hung in the closet. There was no longer any need to hide them from Geary. After all, he was the one who had suggested that Anne work in Blossom Wong's, and now she could use this as an excuse to come and go as she pleased. She had even told him that a chauffeur from Blossom Wong's drove her there and back. The only thing that she had to be careful about was juggling the money when she worked at Blossom Wong's. She had to keep some of it to give to Geary after she saw Yoshi.

Anne was scrubbing the outside of one of the washers that was extremely dirty. The customers were gossiping in Cantonese. Anne's ears were perked, for whenever she was in the laundry she was always listening for the phone. To her, when the call was an invitation from Yoshi's chauffeur, the ring of the phone was almost like a gong in a Chinese opera signaling the beginning of an act. Suddenly, there it was. The phone was ringing.

The chauffeur's harsh voice spoke, "Get ready. Get ready for Yoshi." Anne knew what that meant. She wrote a note for Geary simply saying, "Blossom Wong's tonight." She then finished up in the laundry, put on her Qípáo and was soon standing at Stockton Street and Stark Alley. Some of the women in the laundry had looked at her as if she were a concubine as she passed by the laundry window dressed in her Qípáo but she did not care.

As the Lincoln Town Car roared through the night Anne's heart pounded. Yoshi was waiting. Yoshi was waiting for her.

22

When Anne entered Yoshi's room she saw only a dim light near the dresser. She stood there for a moment, her eyes adjusting to the semi-darkness. Though she could not see him, Anne sensed Yoshi's presence. From somewhere in the room he was watching her. She started to call out his name but thought better of it. She could, of course, try to find a light switch. But Yoshi must have left one dim light on for a reason. She would leave it that way.

Anne began to undress. If he wanted to watch her, let him watch her. She had this feeling that Yoshi did not want a striptease but wanted her to undress in the way she always undressed.

Anne slipped off her Qípáo, enjoying the feel of the silk. She did this as she always did it, slowly, deliberately laying it out as straight as she could, she put it on the carpet. Wiggling her body because it clung to her, she pulled off her slip. She now moved her head forward, reached behind her and unsnapped her bra, then slipped of her panties. Item by item she let fall to the carpet.

Yoshi watched. He liked Anne's unhurried graceful movements. In the dim light she seemed like a shadow of herself. He slowly walked toward Anne. She could feel him approaching.

Yoshi now stood behind Anne. He reached around cupping her breasts, then kissed the nape of her neck. Slowly, almost like a very slow waltz he guided her over to the mirror. Anne watched Yoshi's left hand as his fingers began to tickle her nipple while his right hand slid down her tummy, barely touching her skin. His fingers now circled her belly button. He hesitated a second, then circling and moving down, he lightly brushed against her pubic hair. Anne could now feel the tips of Yoshi's fingers on either side of her labia. He began gently rubbing them back and forth working them against her clitoris. Anne kept watching herself. Watching her heaving breasts, her smile, her dreamy eyes. Yoshi paused. He continued stimulating her clitoris by rubbing her labia back and forth. Pausing, then gently caressing her labia against her clitoris. Finally Anne could feel herself beginning to climax in spite of her wish to hold back. Yoshi sensed this, manipulating her labia, slower, but more rhythmically. Anne could see a tear roll down her cheek. She closed her eyes. Her whole body began to quiver again and again. Finally she was still. Anne looked at herself. She wanted to wipe away the tear from her cheek, but it looked beautiful.

Yoshi now moved back slightly and sat down on the dresser chair. He pulled Anne onto him, kissing her long hair and held her arms outstretched. As Anne worked her buttocks up, down and around trying to please Yoshi as he had pleased her, she kept looking at herself. Finally she could feel his thighs tighten, tighten, then relax.

Anne kept watching herself in the mirror. Watching the beautiful sex-crazed woman who wanted this affair to last and last. Was that her? Was that who she really was?

Yoshi held Anne like that for about twenty minutes. But for her it seemed like they were frozen in time. He then gently pushed her off him and walked toward the bathroom. Anne stood up. She turned around trying to see her back as if she, like the mirror, must see every part of her.

Anne wanted to remain here. She wanted to absorb Yoshi's semen, molecule by molecule. Even his sweat. She wanted to absorb that too.

When she heard Yoshi come out of the bathroom, Anne waited a minute then went to the shower. As the spray washed over her, Yoshi, part of Yoshi was leaving her and running down the drain. But he remained in her heart and in the mirror that had seen them both.

Later when Anne left the hotel she thought the chauffeur looked at her differently, like he now knew her as the mirror knew her, or as others too might now recognize her true Buddha nature.

23

Anne felt a damp chill when she awoke. She heard rain beating against the brick walls of the Quan Shang Laundry and echoing in Stark Alley. She could sense it, but she wanted to be sure. She reached over, Geary was gone. She had her thoughts and her body to herself. She curled up. Yoshi was embracing her. His semen trickled down her thighs. Anne held onto this dream. She floated in and out of consciousness.

All too soon the dream faded. She had to open up the Quan Shang Laundry. Anne put on a pair of Levi's, a black sweater, and an Army field jacket, all clothes that customers had at one time or another left in the laundry. Anne felt comfortable and sexy in these clothes. She liked her Qípáo but she did not need it to make her feel sexy.

As she stepped out into Stark Alley the rain lashed her black hair about her face. If Yoshi were to come by now, he would see the wind having his way with her hair and Yoshi would think it was beautiful. It would be like a bold stroke with the calligraphy brush, the black ink scattering. He would also like the way the raindrops rolled down her cheeks. She caught a glimpse of a dark refection of herself in the window. A bas-relief of her face. Yoshi would appreciate her as a work of art.

Reluctantly Anne opened the door to the laundry. After she had turned on the lights she stepped over to the counter. She could hear her footsteps reverberate. The laundry was like an empty theater only coming to life when customers filled it. Anne remained still for a moment, listening to the rain.

Piled on top of the counter were wash and fold clothes remaining from the night before. Anne sorted them and put them in the washers. A copy of the Asian Week was on one of the sorting tables. Anne thumbed through it. She stopped on page seventeen. There was a beautiful photograph of the black silhouettes of two cranes taken by Wu Shao-Tang. They stood facing each other their beaks raised in the air. The one on the right had its wings spread and appeared to be puffing itself up. Anne assumed this was the male. At first she thought they were getting ready to make love. But looking at it in another way they could as well be getting ready to fight. Perhaps the red background was a giveaway, for in China red means good things are going to happen.

Anne had no sooner turned the page to the Miss Chinatown contest than she heard the front door open. She looked up. It was Mrs. Teng. She was wearing a three-quarter length yellow raincoat and was pushing a laundry cart covered with a black plastic bag.

"I have to keep busy. Even on a day like this," Mrs. Teng said, as if she had been asked for an explanation.

"Oh checking out the competition." Mrs. Teng observed, looking at the page showing the photos of the women entered in the Miss Chinatown contest.

"Not exactly," Anne replied. "I was thumbing through the pages, and I just happened to..."

"Things don't just happen you know. You were thinking of your boyfriend, sizing up the competition."

"I am married, Mrs. Teng."

"So? I see through your mask. It is written all over your face that you have a boyfriend. Even the way you walk. I see you clearly."

Anne took a deep breath, not knowing what to say.

"Don't worry. Your mask is safe with me. But watch out. Hide behind it as well as you can."

Anne let her breath out slowly.

"Well. I certainly had a strange time last night, quite sexy too," Mrs. Teng said as she began stuffing her clothes into the washers.

"As usual," Anne remarked.

"I dreamt I was dancing in a nightclub with a big strong man. The orchestra was playing 'Summertime' and there were soft lights."

Anne snickered. She was hardly surprised.

"Afterwards he led me to a corner booth. He began feeling me up, then pulling off my clothes. Next we were on the floor. 'Summertime' was still playing. His thick semen ran down my thighs. I couldn't resist. I couldn't resist."

Mrs. Teng had said this in such a way as if she expected Anne to ask Why?

"Why?" Anne asked thinking that the response would be that all big strong man are irresistible.

"Because he was Chairman Mao."

"Chairman Mao?" Anne had hardly expected this answer. "Well Mrs. Teng," Anne said. "Knowing you, you could easily have said 'no' but of course you do have a weakness."

"I could not have said no," Mrs. Teng said emphatically. "If Chairman Mao can conquer all China, he can certainly conquer me. Even in my dreams."

"But Chairman Mao is dead," Anne reminded her.

"So what? He came to me in my dream. And he will come again. I know it. He was as real as any man. More. When I woke up, I was having an orgasm, and I was wet between my thighs. I am Chairman Mao's concubine," Mrs. Teng said proudly. "He is the best lover I ever had."

Anne started to laugh.

"Don't laugh," Mrs. Teng said. "I have had good sex with all of them. Attila the Hun, Genghis Khan, Kublai Khan, and Chairman Mao. He is the one with the biggest cock."

Anne wondered if Mrs. Teng was all right in the head.

Reading her thoughts Mrs. Teng replied, "Certain men have power over women. Even in death. They remain in our dreams. They glide between our thighs."

Anne looked outside. The rain was keeping the other customers away. Just as well. She enjoyed listening to Mrs. Teng alone.

One thing she wondered, perhaps it could work the other way too. She had exerted her sexual power over Yoshi and he had succumbed. She would conquer all Japan until the Rising Sun lay at her feet.

24

Anne was in the back of the laundry when she heard the phone ring. As she made her way through the customers and laundry carts, she thought she heard a woman's voice say, "boyfriend," but with the noise of the washers, dryers, and the din of loud conversations, she could not be sure. Someone may have seen her leave with the chauffeur and assumed the truth. Or they may have even been referring to someone else. Anyway, gossips were everywhere especially in Chinatown, but life went on nonetheless.

Anne picked up the phone. A woman gave her an intense look, or was Anne reading too much into her gaze? Hopefully, the phone call was from Yoshi's chauffeur telling her he would pick her up. The phone was silent. Had the other party hung up? Did she miss the chauffeur's call? Then, just as Anne was about to hang up, she heard Blossom Wong's voice. "I need you as soon as you can come. A man is sick."

A man is sick. Why not take him to a doctor or an acupuncturist? Anne thought.

"I know a good acupuncturist," Anne replied.

"No, I need you now. Come as you are."

"Give me a minute to wrap things up."

A little later when Anne left the laundry, she could imagine all kinds of things being said behind her back. Little old men and women venting the frustrations of their dull lives. Anne argued with herself. If that was true, so what? Or perhaps it was more mundane. There were always gossips. Some people paid attention to them, but most went about their lives, simply being entertained by a story which they soon forgot.

As Anne walked down Stockton Street, she enjoyed the noises and smells of Chinatown. She inhaled the aroma of Peking duck, of roasted pigs, Szechwan prawns,... she heard children playing and grandmothers scolding, couples arguing and making love. Chinatown was a delight, a feast of noises and smells. In contrast Quincy Alley was so silent that one could hear water running down the drainpipes outside the walls of its old brick buildings. No children played there. No flowers grew. On the right side of a doorway there was a sign written in gold Chinese characters. Few people knew it for what it really was.

Although Anne worked at Blossom Wong's she still had to go through the ritual of knocking on the door, waiting for the bouncer to open the peephole, then waiting a few more minutes until he slowly opened the door. Everyone had to go through this ritual except Blossom Wong. But she owned the building. She made the rituals.

When the door finally closed behind her the bouncer said, "Blossom Wong wants to see you in her room."

Anne knocked apprehensively. "Come in. Come in," Blossom Wong said in her charming voice. "Here, have a seat next to me." Anne quickly looked around the room before sitting down. There was a beautiful Chinese landscape painting, a bed with a thick dark green comforter, a samovar on a brass table, a screen inlaid with jade showing various court scenes and a large jade statue of the Buddha on a low table in front of Blossom Wong. Also on it was a Chinese novel which apparently Blossom Wong was reading. The room was simple, yet very refined.

"My dear San San," Blossom Wong said. "Shanghai was such a beautiful city in the 30's. I remember my father's chauffeur driving us in the Packard along the Bund. There were so many colorful junks in the water. Anyway, to get to my point. My old boyfriend from those days, Chung Chi Fung is very sick. Perhaps you can help him."

Old boyfriend? Anne thought. *He is probably one of many.* And if he were sick, wouldn't he need a doctor or an acupuncturist as she had told Blossom Wong on the phone?

"Perhaps I should elaborate," Blossom Wong said sensing Anne's reservations. "He has headaches, and his hearing is failing. Sometimes we do cures here."

Do cures here? Anne wondered. Curing what? Making soft penises hard? But headaches and bad hearing?

"Don't be skeptical," Blossom Wong said reading Anne's thoughts. "I learned these cures in Shanghai for bad hearing, headaches, arthritis, and much more. You'll see."

"By the way, you need not get a Qípáo from the closet. Your friends will be in room four. They will have something for you."

Blossom Wong turned slightly away and began to read the novel that was on the table.

As Anne left, she mused, *I'm supposed to cure headaches and bad hearing. What's next?*

Anne slowly turned the handle of room four. Was she to be the go-down girl again?

"Here she is," the woman with high cheekbones announced.

"The go-down girl?" Anne said smiling faintly. She certainly did not want to be seen as taking herself too seriously.

"My name is Yan Yun as you probably know. We are all familiar from last time." Anne saw the same women and the same musical instruments on the table. Was this going to be a repeat performance?

"As you know," Yan Yun said. "Blossom Wong's old boyfriend is losing his hearing and has headaches. She says this is due to sexual disharmonies."

Yes. Yes. Anne thought. *And the only thing that will set him right is a good go-down girl.*

Yan Yun continued, "Chung Chi Fung needs more of the female element to bring him into sexual harmony."

What man doesn't? Anne thought.

"Blossom Wong said this cure is thousands of years old and that she received it in secret," Yan Yun explained.

Blow jobs, if that's what it is, must go back further that that, Anne thought, *and they are certainly no secret.*

"Listen carefully to me San San," Yan Yun said, "while I describe what we are going to do."

Anne listened attentively.

"Now before we go into the other room we will take off our clothes and put on the embroidered silk blouses behind you."

Anne turned around there were several silk blouses on wooden hangers each one beautifully embroidered. She reached for a green blouse embroidered with small red flowers. Anne removed her sweater and began to put the blouse on over her bra.

"No, you must first undress completely," Yan Yun said sharply.

Anne was surprised to hear Yan Yun speak with such authority. She hesitated for a minute, then began taking off all her clothes. The other women did likewise, even Yan Yun herself.

Anne put on the green embroidered silk blouse which felt wonderful against her breasts, almost like Yoshi's hands. The other women were putting on their blouses. Did they too like the way the silk caressed their breasts?

"Leave your blouses unbuttoned," Yan Yun ordered.

"Everybody ready?" she asked. Yan Yun did not wait for an answer. They filed out of the door and walked down the hallway almost in lock step with Yan Yun leading. Anne watched her firm buttocks tightening and slackening.

Yan Yun opened a door and held it as they all trooped in. Anne was the last to enter.

"Now remember what I told you," Yan Yun said and then gave Anne a soft pat on her right buttock.

Although Anne had heard Blossom Wong say that Chung Chi Fung was an old boyfriend "from those days in Shanghai," she was still surprised when she saw an old man two inches or more shorter than herself, with thinning gray hair. He stooped, though he tried to stand as erect as he could. He was dressed in a dark double-breasted suit with a vest and a gold watch chain. He certainly looked like he was from the Shanghai of the 30's.

Anne kept contrasting in her mind Chung Chi Fung's appearance with that of Blossom Wong's. While he seemed old, bent, and unsmiling, Blossom Wong stood up straight, and had a spring in her step, and her skin was soft and pliant due to a lifetime of using expensive creams and a healthy diet. Also her mind was young and alert. What had she seen in this man who seemed like he had always been this way? It was not hard to imagine Blossom Wong as a vivacious young woman going to parties in Shanghai.

"Gracious ladies," Chung Chi Fung said in a cracked voice, bowing slightly. "I appreciate your help." He took an intense look at their almost naked bodies, then slowly knelt down on a cushion before what appeared to be a Daoist scroll.

Well, he certainly still seems to have keen eyesight, Anne thought to herself.

The woman who had played the Xiäo sat on a low chair and began very softly. The woman who had played the Yuèqín chimed.

"A man who is hard of hearing should have very tranquil music during the cure," Yan Yun had explained earlier. "He needs inner peace."

Anne stood there enjoying listening to the Xiäo.

The woman who had previously played the Húgín knelt down, unzipped the man's pants and began to suck on his penis.

Oh yes the cure-all, Anne thought.

"San San, remember your role," Yan Yun said sharply.

Reluctantly Anne pressed her pussy against Chung Chi Fung's right ear. This was supposed to cure his bad hearing? How boring.

To occupy her mind Anne read the scroll.

THE DAO OF PURE AND CLUTTERED MIND

Pure mind is like a flowing river

Always subtly changing course

Cluttered mind is like a river with myriad forks

Eventually it becomes swamp and quagmire

***

The direction of pure mind is like the course

Wherein the river flows - the way of the flow

Cluttered mind is like a stagnant stream

Whereupon a leaf meanders aimlessly

***

Pure mind is unhurried as a river is unhurried

It flows quickly or slowly according to the course

Cluttered mind is like a river in torrent

Surging wildly, then bogging down with rubbish

***

Pure mind knows no bounds

It is the river and its course

Cluttered mind surges over embankments
Or bogs down and evaporates

***

Pure mind is simple
It is one river replenishing the sea
Cluttered mind is forked. It is consumed, vaporized
Before it reaches the sea. It never replenishes

***

Pure mind is deep. However you try to fathom it
Your line moves the way of the flow
Cluttered mind is shallow
Any fool can plummet his line therein

***

Pure mind is like a crystal mirror reflecting clearly
Cluttered mind is like shattered glass, reflecting poorly, scattering images

***

Anne's mind felt in a tranquil state, uncluttered. Just then Yan Yun bent forward, reached under Anne's blouse, and pinched her nipple lightly. She then pressed her lips against Anne's and quickly slid her tongue under Anne's front lip, then moved her head away.

"Get with it," she whispered in Anne's ear.

A bolt of sexual energy surged through Anne. Whereas previously she had almost passively scrunched her pussy against Chung Chi Fung's right ear, she now pressed against it firmly all the while looking into Yan Yun's deep black eyes. It was as if Yan Yun were the man, and she were the woman and keeping in tempo with the Xiäo and the Yuèqín they were making love. Their sexual energy, almost like electricity, was being transmitted through Chung Chi Fung's head, from one ear to the other. Anne continued looking into Yan Yun's eyes, only now they seemed soft and compliant and hers intent, narrowed. She was now the man and Yan Yun the woman. She could feel herself being overwhelmed, climaxing and Yan Yun kissing her, climaxing. Their sexual energies flowing through Chung Chi Fung's gray-haired head, and his out of his penis and into the go-down girl's mouth.

Silence. Pure mind was at rest. The go-down girl took a handkerchief, wiped off Chung Chi Fung's penis, and zipped up his pants. He remained on his knees, reading the Daoist scroll.

"Pure mind is like a flowing river."

As they walked down the hallway toward room four Yan Yun turned toward Anne and said, "San San, Chung Chi Fung is cured. We will be well paid."

"How do you know?" Anne asked skeptically.

"Because qì energy passed through his head. I was a man and you were a woman. And you were a man and I was a woman, passing our sexual energies back and forth through his head. Before that happened, he was merely having fun and so were we. It doesn't always happen you know. Only some women have that power together, and then not always."

Anne thought about it. A man's headaches and bad hearing had been cured by two women rubbing their pussies against his ears and having an orgasm. Was it true? Why not? But what's next? Bad eyesight? Nasal problems? Tongue problems?

Pure mind is like a flowing river

Pure mind knows no bounds

Pure mind is deep

Pure mind.

25

Anne often passed the Peng Fei Antique Shop when she went shopping on Stockton Street. At first, she hardly noticed it. Perhaps this was because as she looked through the window it was so full that her eyes did not fix on any one thing. There were antique jade Buddhas, chairs, tables, scrolls, screens, vases, and much more. Although these items were laid out neatly enough, they were not laid out in a particular order, such as certain types of furniture together, then a space, then the screens and so on. In fact, except for the aisle leading to the counter in the back, there were no spaces, there were no divisions.

At first, like the store, Anne had hardly noticed him. But just as the store had intrigued her more and more as she looked through the window and became more and more aware of its contents, so, too, with the proprietor who sat in the back. He was hardly noticeable for he wore a black skullcap and a black robe with long flowing sleeves. He had a thin gray beard, almost white, and sat in a high-backed chair in front of a small desk. Occasionally he puffed on a long-stemmed pipe. His chair and desk were slightly to the side of the aisle and because of the coloring of his clothes, he appeared to someone strolling by as an anonymous dark form, almost like a black curtain, that hung in the back of the shop.

Whenever Anne passed the Peng Fei Antique Shop she usually noticed something that she had not been aware of before, like the day she had seen an ancient Chinese hanging scroll.

On another day, she looked in hoping to see the old man, for he was not always there, and was delighted to see him bent over his desk on which was laid out a long white piece of paper, making quick smooth strokes with a calligraphy brush. Anne could not quite see the characters, but she suspected he could make them more elegantly than most Chinese scholars nowadays, for he was definitely of the old school.

She was about to continue when she noticed, in the corner of the window, characters drawn on a long white strip of paper. As she stepped over to inspect it, she could tell that the paper was grainier and appeared thicker than any that she had ever seen for sale, even in China. The calligraphy was exquisite, almost of museum quality, and what had been written was quite beautiful, yet amusing: May the Buddha be with you.

May you see through the labyrinth. Was he talking about her looking through the maze of the objects in the store; yet something deeper too? She thought he looked up and smiled at her, but she wasn't sure. It had happened so quickly, and her eyes had been focused on the small scroll. She could hardly imagine such a serious looking scholar doing anything in jest.

The characters were strong, bold. They had a haunting quality to them which made them linger in her mind.

Several days went by until Anne again passed the Peng Fei Antique Shop. As she approached the window, she looked through the tables, chairs, and vases. Things seemed rearranged through she could not tell exactly how. This was not the first time that she had noticed this. Perhaps something had been sold. Or, in order to clean a vase or some other item, the proprietor had moved something, for every item in the store was dusted and polished as if new. Whoever bought things here must be extremely wealthy and have good taste.

As usual Anne looked for the old scholar, but he was not sitting in his chair. No, there was a Chinese boy about eight sitting in it, dressed in a Catholic school uniform. He was bent over the desk doing calligraphy. Anne took another step. There was the old scholar standing behind the boy, apparently giving him instructions. An old man instructing his grandson. For a moment, the boy stopped. The old man took the brush out of his hand and slowly drew a character. The boy waited as the old scholar drew the character, then drew one beneath it. He then, as far as Anne could tell, continued copying his lessons. Anne wondered to herself: Why was the boy going to Catholic school? The old scholar was undoubtedly the patriarch of his family, and the word of such a man in a Chinese family was law.

The old scholar could have insisted that the boy be raised a Buddhist. Though perhaps he was being raised as a Buddhist and was merely attending Catholic school. Anne felt this was the case, though she had no proof of it.

Anne was about to leave when she glanced at the calligraphy and poem that was usually posted in the upper-right-hand corner of the window. There was a new aphorism: The long way is the short way, and another next to it: The river flows between the rocks.

These maxims looked as if they had been written recently, as if for her benefit. They seemed both serious and humorous. The calligraphy itself also gave them power. While the little Japanese calligraphy Anne had seen seemed smooth, rounded, the Chinese calligraphy as she contrasted it in her mind, was angular, stark, as if it were reality itself. Chinese calligraphy had a power and strength that Japanese calligraphy did not. Chinese calligraphy was dominant and Japanese civilization would succumb.

The old scholar looked up at her. He did not smile.

26

The chauffeur phoned. Anne was quite glad to leave her husband and the laundry. Quickly but not quickly enough she was soon on her way to the Hotel Kabuki. She entered Yoshi's room as if she were, yes, Yoshi's mistress. The woman who needed no explaining.

Anne had decided that she had Yoshi pretty well figured out. She took some mascara out of her purse and starting from her right side just below her bellybutton she drew the Chinese character for tiger, and below that the one for hare, and below that the one for dragon. Although she had, for reasons even she herself did not know, chosen characters that represented years in the Chinese calendar there was no meaning in the sense of a sentence for the characters she had drawn on herself. She now turned around and faced Yoshi. Had she sized him up correctly?

Yoshi looked at the characters that Anne had drawn on herself. He smiled broadly, then led her to the bed. As she lay on the bed Yoshi kissed each character: the tiger, the hare, and the dragon. Anne could feel Yoshi's hands gently spread her thighs apart. His hot tongue glided inside her, slowly circled, he stopped, kissed her clitoris, circled inside, kissed her clitoris, again and again until she climaxed. Until the tiger, the hare, and the dragon trembled.

Anne lay there quietly for a moment, then began laughing. Yoshi had done just as she thought he would. He had interpreted the characters which he couldn't read and really had no meaning as a sentence as if they were an invitation for him to devour her. She snuggled up to Yoshi. She knew him well. She had him in her power.

Were there other things Anne would do to manipulate Yoshi? Of course. *Of course*, Anne thought. She went over to the dresser, and on her left side, starting a little higher than her bellybutton Anne slowly drew the same characters as she had drawn on her right side but in reverse order. So that they now read: Dragon. Hare. Tiger. Yoshi watched fascinated as Anne slowly drew the characters on herself. Yoshi lay down on the bed. His fingers pressed into her thighs as he pulled them toward him. Anne lingered above Yoshi's face, letting him see into her, before devouring her essence. She pressed herself hard against his face feeling his tongue in her and on her clitoris. Anne now reciprocated. Kissing Yoshi's penis, savoring it, letting it slide against her tongue. She looked at the mirror on the dresser. Her black hair looked like a brush stroke guided by Yoshi's penis, as if invisible characters were being drawn on him. Perhaps they were. Perhaps that was what this was all about. Anne tasted Yoshi. She tasted the black ink.

Anne lay on top of Yoshi. She thought about how their bellybuttons were together. The place where each of them had been tied off from their mothers and had then been wound back into themselves. Her thought was as real as the silkworm. Anne clung to this image, then it vanished.

As they now sat on the edge of the bed. Anne felt sad. Soon Yoshi would put on his business suit and head for Silicon Valley, and she would put on her Qípáo and return to the laundry. They would be as separated as the characters she had drawn on herself.

Anne had not had memory enough. When her lover left in the Chinese opera did not the woman wave with her fan? Did she not wish him a last farewell? Anne had choreographed their love-night so far. She would continue with the script. She walked slowly over to the dresser, picked up the mascara, and drew the character for the rat on her left breast and for the ox on her right one. She picked up the fan which she had left there earlier. She turned around and as delicately as she could she moved the fan from her left breast to the right one, then stopped. Yoshi gazed at her breasts as if he had never seen them before. He put each nipple in his mouth, tasting it. Did not the characters compel him to do this? The fan had moved across her breasts, revealing each character slowly. There was a truth there that must be savored. Anne looked down at Yoshi, kissing and fondling one breast, then the other. He had succumbed to her every desire. That was the way she wanted to remember him.

The rat, the ox, the tiger, the hare, and the dragon. Five years had passed in the Chinese calendar and Yoshi had savored each one of them.

27

"I can't make it," Geary said.

"Why? You promised we would go together," Anne replied.

"Look, I'm working late. There's a car I've got to have ready by tomorrow morning. Don't bother with dinner. I'll eat out."

Anne started to say something, but Geary hung up the phone. Who was he kidding? Working

late? Did he expect her to believe that? She had heard music in the background, and the sound of men and women laughing. He was probably at the Club Hong Kong again, or some other low dive. He had promised he would take her to the Chinese New Year parade. She had closed the laundry early and was now sitting alone in the kitchen with the night before her. If only Yoshi were here lying in the bed with a hard cock that she could tease with her tongue. Well, he wasn't and there wasn't much she could do about it other than roll her tongue around in her mouth and suck on it. What time was it in Japan? What was Yoshi doing now? She imagined him in a nice neat busy office. She did not want to think of him in the arms of his wife or between the legs of another woman.

Anne got up to go to bed. She had no sooner taken a few steps, than she stopped. Geary was out. She was a grown woman. She could do as she wished. She did not need Geary to accompany her to the Chinese New Year's parade, though it would have been nice to do something together for once, for they had been married for over a year now and they had not gone out together. But as she thought about it, maybe it was just as well that she went alone. She was soon out the door and on her way.

Anne was surprised, though she should not have been, that so many other Chinese, both single and in families were also on the way to see the New Year's parade. There was the grandfather pushing his granddaughter in a pram. She was standing up in it, eating a piece of fried fish, the grease running down her fat rosy cheeks. There were also single women just like her. Anne thought that maybe they too had marital problems or boyfriend problems. She hoped not; but the reality of life was that in this she was not alone. Mostly there were families. Several children were holding onto a rope, slung over the shoulder of a matronly woman, probably their aunt. Parents and grandparents followed behind, laughing and joking. A boy wearing a blue coat and blue hat sat on his father's shoulders, overlooking all, almost like a little emperor.

Finally they reached Grant Avenue. Masses of Chinese were stretched out on either side of the street. They spoke and swore in Cantonese of various dialects, and in Mandarin. Some were short, others were tall, and some were old and bent. Above them leaning over the balconies of their apartment houses topped with pagodas and steep sloping tiled roofs were families, waving and talking to their friends below. Their children threw small firecrackers into the crowd. People yelled up at them, but the children were not punished or scolded.

These were her people, stretching back from the Qing dynasty, the Ming, the Yuan, the Song... and back to the Shang. Conquerors like Genghis Khan had come, and they had succumbed to Chinese civilization.

Anne heard the beating of drums, and the clanging of cymbals. She looked down Grant Avenue and saw it snaking up the street, a red dragon, its head moving to and fro, emitting invisible fire, propelled by what seemed like a thousand human feet. Everyone laughed and shouted, and more firecrackers were thrown down.

All Chinese knew its power. Invaders like the Mongols, the Yuan Dynasty, had come and gone and the dragon had devoured them one by one in the belly of Chinese civilization.

The dragon snaked past her. Anne followed it, bumping into people, until she bumped into an old man who shook his fist at her. "Young people have no respect," he shouted. The crowd was now too dense, and besides she had seen what she had wanted to see. She turned away and walked up Sacramento Street.

Anne mused to herself: China was like a red dragon that was like a woman absorbing the invader's semen in her mouth and in her vagina until he lay subdued at her feet. This image gave her an idea; and that idea led to another idea.

28

Anne walked down Stockton Street, looking in each jewelry store for a red jade dragon. She stopped in front of Cheng's Jewelry Company. There were beautiful jade bracelets and Piaget watches, but no red jade dragon. She looked in jewelry shop after jewelry shop, then when she was just about to give up, she looked in one last jewelry shop window and there it was, not one but a good twenty or more red jade dragons. All in slightly different shades of red. Anne glanced at the sign: Eternity Jewelry written on the window in Chinese characters.

Anne opened the door. A woman about her age was behind the counter looking at a diamond through a jeweler's magnifying lens.

"I'd like to see the tray of red dragons," Anne asked. The woman removed the magnifying lens as if she were happy to be seeing with both eyes again. "These just arrived from China for the Year of the Dragon," she said as she put the tray on the counter. Anne looked through the tray, picking up several pieces. Finally, she picked out one that was the brightest red, wishing it was redder still.

"I'll take this one," Anne said, pointing.

"A wise choice and beautiful too," the woman said. "And how will you wear it?"

Anne hadn't thought of that. The jeweler pointed to a gold chain.

"Perhaps silver," Anne said, thinking of the price.

"Are you sure? The colors don't go well together."

"Here, I will show you."

The jeweler put the red dragon on the silver chain and around Anne's neck. The woman's fingers felt warm and soothing as she lightly touched the back of Anne's neck. For some reason Anne had a vision of the woman using this as a ruse to choke someone she didn't like. The jeweler now held a mirror in front of Anne. Yes, the woman was right. The silver chain did not seem to go well with the red dragon. The jeweler quickly replaced the silver chain with a gold one. Anne looked at herself again in the mirror... at the red dragon hanging from the gold chain.

That was it. The red and the gold complemented each other. The gold seemed to bring out the true color of the red jade.

"You were certainly right," Anne said. "Yes, I'll take them."

"I am always right," the woman answered. "About jewelry, that is. I am almost always wrong about men though," she said, laughing.

"That will be $112.58. Trust me, I am good at mental arithmetic."

Anne took a hundred and a twenty-dollar bill from her purse. She always had a few hundred dollars or more from Blossom Wong's. Why had she even thought of being cheap?

"Here is a case," the jeweler said as she handed Anne the change. It was a small black case with yellow cloth lining. Impulsively Anne put it in her purse.

"I will wear the red dragon for the rest of the day," Anne stated.

"Careful," the jeweler replied.

"Yes," Anne said. "I will not wear it for my husband. I will not let him see it."

The woman smiled as if she had known that all along. As Anne left the Eternity Jewelry store, she was conscious of the red dragon hanging from the gold chain. Though no one paid any attention to her, she felt a new power.

29

Anne never knew how long it would be between Yoshi's visits. Sometimes many weeks. Sometimes months. She was quite surprised then when only two weeks passed until the chauffeur phoned again. Hurriedly, without even bothering to tell Geary, Anne closed the laundry early and left with the chauffeur for the Hotel Kabuki.

She was soon in Yoshi's room. She walked right past him as he stood there bewildered, slipped off her clothes, and stepped into the shower. Several minutes later she felt Yoshi's hand on her shoulder. She turned around, reached over and let her hand slide down his chest.

Anne wanted to feel Yoshi's body. She wanted to feel every muscle in his body. Anne adjusted the shower. Previously she had bought some Yardley's lavender soap. She pressed down on the cap, soaping her hands. She rubbed her fingertips against Yoshi's well-muscled chest, feeling his ribs. She felt them expand and contract. Yoshi stood there, his rippling stomach muscles facing her. Anne wondered if that was why when his penis was erect it was so hard and stuck up so high. Did his stomach muscles have something to do with it? Her husband's stomach was flabby. Aside from the fact that it was ugly and pressed down on her when they had sex she wondered if his droopy stomach didn't cause his droopy penis which she sometimes had to suck to attention.

Anne smiled at Yoshi as she put more soap on her hands and began rubbing them on his stomach. As she rubbed she pressed against it, feeling her hands glide over each muscle which relaxed for a second, then sprang back into place. While doing this Anne spoke in Cantonese saying, "I like your stomach muscles. I like the way they hold up your penis." And more such things. Yoshi who of course spoke no Cantonese, thoroughly enjoyed listening to the sounds of Anne's soft voice as her hands glided over his skin. Anne now soaped Yoshi's penis and testicles. How wonderful and alive they felt. Much more so than her husband's and her boyfriend Ling Chiao's. No, at this moment she did not want to even think about him.

Anne kneaded Yoshi's thighs. Her hands pressed deeply into them, feeling their strength. Yoshi turned around. Anne's fingers glided over his back muscles feeling their power. Yoshi now put soap on his hands. She felt electricity from them as his hands traced her body. He pressed himself against her. Their soapy bodies glided against each other. Anne could feel the shower tingling against her skin as she curled her toes tightly.

Afterward Anne took the towel and began drying off Yoshi, rubbing the towel hard and quickly against his skin so that she could almost feel electricity coming from it. Then she also dried herself off briskly. She pressed herself against his back pushing her breasts against him, feeling the electricity between their bodies.

Soon they were on the bed. Anne climbed on Yoshi. Her red jade dragon hung down in front of Yoshi's face. He watched it like a cat watching a pendulum, as it swung back and forth between her breasts. Yoshi extended his hands. The tips of his fingers tickled her nipples. She pressed her hands against his shoulders feeling his muscles, tightening her fingers until her nails dug into him like claws. Yoshi watched the swaying red dragon lower and lower. Soon its sharp edges raked against his skin while he ejaculated into the depths. Why was he here? Why was he in this room? Why was he in this woman's power?

30

Yoshi drummed his fingers lightly on his desk. His mind drifted. He was tickling San San's pussy. His fingers paused, then rubbed the desk, just barely pressing against it. What was he doing? He was supposed to be receiving a fax, but in his mind, he was in the hotel in San Francisco with San San. She was so turned on by him that she was just about to suck his penis.

Wait. Wasn't he supposed to be a Japanese businessman totally absorbed in his work? But lately that was all there was to his life. Work, work, and more work. He hardly knew his daughter or his wife. He seldom went drinking with his friends. Okamoto Electronics was his world, yet he had to have his dreams and his dream mistress.

There. There was the fax coming in. It was in German. How did anybody understand that language? It seemed only suited for giving orders. His fingers rubbed against San San's pussy again, then he called his secretary over.

"Well, what does the fax say?" Yoshi asked his secretary. "I'm sure we'll recover most of the money from the shipping insurance company."

Yoshi's secretary picked up the fax and started to read it, translating from German.

Dear Mr. Yoshi Okamoto:

The Schlegel Insurance Company has received the manifests of your losses from Hansa Shipping Lines. As to the first part of your claim... the crates and boxes from your firm were loaded into forty-eight-foot containers. However, Hansa Lines ships, like those of many shipping lines, can only stow twenty- and forty-foot containers below deck. The below deck cells will not accommodate forty-eight-foot containers. Therefore, your containers were stowed on deck and subsequently lost in Hurricane Blanc. This loss was entirely due to your firm's not using forty-foot containers.

Secondly, as you know, Schlegel Insurance is a new firm and is also known as Get Clout Insurance.com located in Menlo Park, California, which recently declared bankruptcy. Therefore, our capital is limited. You will only be paid 10,000 marks. The money will be wired to your firm's account shortly.

Further inquiries should be made to Get Clout Insurance.com

Sincerely,

Hans von Ebenhardt

"Please translate the fax for me again," Yoshi asked his secretary. "Perhaps a little slower this time."

His secretary read the fax again, slowly, in the same flat, unemotional tone of voice as before. Her face gave no indication as to how she felt. After his secretary had finished Yoshi sat there in silence. His secretary sensed that he wanted to be alone and walked back to her desk.

10,000 marks. An insult really. Not enough to keep his firm afloat even for a day or so. But before panicking he would look into what went wrong. He needed to speak with Mr. Hakamada who was in charge of shipping. This would not be easy. He pressed Mr. Hakamada's extension number.

"This is Mr. Hakamada, Director of Shipping. I would be very honored to help you."

"Thank you," Yoshi began, his tone of voice sounding a bit more refined than he felt comfortable with. "This is Mr. Yoshi Okamoto. Perhaps I can see you in an hour."

"I would be delighted to meet with you, honorable president," Mr. Hakamada replied.

So like Mr. Hakamada, Yoshi thought, a true gentlemen of the old school. He had been a young lieutenant under Admiral Yamamoto during the war. In his own mind he was, however, still in the Japan before World War II. For instance, one of his hobbies which he often practiced at work was calligraphy and both he and his wife belonged to an Ikebana flower arranging society. Both had won several awards. He wasn't too bad at origami either and evidence of his work could often be found on his desk.

Had Mr. Hakamada not been with the firm when Yoshi had taken it over, Yoshi would never have hired him, for he lived entirely in the past. Previously he had not even believed in using a computer or a telephone though he now had to have them. Perhaps it was because he wanted his office to have a Zen-like appearance which it certainly with careful arrangement still had: a clean desk with a computer and a few stacks of letters placed here and there on his desk just as one arranged flowers in an Ikebana flower arrangement or a Zen garden. On the wall were a few family photos.

When Yoshi had taken over the firm, which was then quite small, nobody despite the awe and respect Yoshi and the other employees had for him, thought Mr. Hakamada would adapt. Yoshi was determined to go "hi-tech." However, Mr. Hakamada had surprised everyone, perhaps even himself. He had gone to school at night and learned computers. His progress was perhaps uneven, but it was sure and after little more than a year he was using them with greater facility than anyone in the office, even helping the other employees. Because of his naval experience he had gravitated toward shipping and had until now certainly made the department more modern and economical.

Yoshi stood in front of Mr. Hakamada's door which was slightly ajar. He knocked as lightly as he could. Mr. Hakamada opened the door slowly, majestically, as if he were receiving royalty or a superior officer. He bowed slightly. "It is an honor to see you Mr. President."

"Mr. Hakamada, it is always an honor to see one who has served our country," Yoshi replied.

Mr. Hakamada tensed. Though he never spoke of it in any way, he felt a personal responsibility for losing the war. While even he knew it could not be entirely his fault he felt it deeply nonetheless.

"Please be seated," Yoshi said. "May I?" Yoshi asked, pointing to a seat.

"It would please me," Mr. Hakamada replied.

Yoshi sat down. The computer was placed on Mr. Hakamada's desk in such a position so as to be like a well-placed stone in a Zen monastery garden. There were three stacks of letters, none as high as the others, laid on the desk as if they were rectangular stone slabs in this garden. There was even a white origami crane placed as if drinking from a brook. Off to the right side of the desk was the telephone and just a little from it a small Ikebana flower arrangement, almost like the gateway to the garden. On the wall were some photographs. One of Mr. Hakamada as a young naval officer. Another of him in his naval officer's uniform and his wife next to him in a kimono and traditional hairdo. There were two other photographs: one of his son when he was about three and another of his daughter when she was about the same age. Yoshi wondered why there were no photographs of them when they were adults, but guessed, quite correctly, though he did not know it, that they dressed and acted in the modern manner and Mr. Hakamada did not approve.

Although Mr. Hakamada was Yoshi's employee, Yoshi felt intimidated by this man who was the embodiment of Japan's past. For a few moments he was speechless, trying to think of how to begin. "Mr. Hakamada," Yoshi started in almost a whisper, "I understand that you switched from shipping in forty-foot containers to forty-eight-foot ones." Yoshi tried to lengthen his sentence, to make it a little more flowery, but nothing further came out of his mouth.

"Yes," Mr. Hakamada replied, proudly. "I searched with my computer and found that by switching to them we could save considerably if we shipped in enough volume, which we do."

"We also changed shipping companies and insurance companies," Yoshi added.

"As you said," Mr. Hakamada answered. "We must be realistic in this day and age, and not overly sentimental if we are to maximize profits. So I switched from Tokyo Express Shipping Lines to Hansa Shipping Lines and from Lloyd's of London to Schegel Insurance. Perhaps I should have switched sooner. I'm a bit sentimental I'm afraid."

"No, no," Yoshi said. "Your feelings were in the right place."

Yoshi had admit to himself that by his words and his very attitude he had conveyed the impression that he was willing to try any new system, yes, including dot.com start-ups solely for a profit with bragging rights. Previous to this frenzy which was beginning to grip Japan, and indeed the whole world, his company had been profiting more and more each year. But now he was chasing everybody else and they were chasing him. Previously he had time for his wife and daughter. He hadn't even gone to the sumo wrestling matches with his friends in over a year. Mr. Hakamada for all his quaintness had kept shipping costs down, probably through his old naval connections though Yoshi never asked him how he did it. Technically, Yoshi should reprimand him. He could not bring himself to do this. Instead, Yoshi found himself saying rather stiffly, "It is always a pleasure to speak with you Mr. Hakamada. By the way, how is your Go game?"

"I seem to be slipping in my old age. I know more, but mere knowledge is not enough. These younger players."

Yoshi was amused though he did not show it. By younger Mr. Hakamada was referring to men in their forties or fifties. Also, he was being far too modest. He was a fourth dan and not to be trifled with.

"Well, you have more than enough fighting spirit to overcome them."

Yoshi stood up. Mr. Hakamada rose, standing stiffly almost like he was standing at attention in front of a superior officer.

"Please give me my regards to Mrs. Hakamada and your family," Yoshi said.

"Yes Mr. President, and please give my regards to Mrs. Okamoto and your family."

Both men bowed slightly. Yoshi now turned to leave. He looked back for a second, only to see Mr. Hakamada looking at his ikebana flower arrangement as if that were the only reality for him.

31

"You must come by. You must come by." Blossom Wong said in a light lilting voice. "It'll be lots of fun. It'll be fabulous. Of course you won't be making any money."

"I have to make something otherwise my husband will get suspicious," Anne replied.

"Well, I could give you $200."

"I don't think I could accept."

"Nonsense, if I want to give you $200. I will give it to you. You will not question me."

"No, never." Anne laughed.

"You will come then?"

"Yes. Yes."

"Come about seven. That way you'll have plenty of time to get fixed up for the party. I call it

'Shanghai Night.'"

Anne was soon out of the door and on her way. Money, that was her ticket. As she approached Quincy Alley she saw a large old-fashioned car turn into the alley. A chauffeur, but not Yoshi's chauffeur, thank goodness, opened the door. A Chinese man stepped out. He had wide lapels on his suit, and pants pressed with a razor-sharp crease. His shoes were white with black leather trimmings. *Why would anyone dress like it was 1930?* Anne wondered. She hung back while the man knocked on the door. Almost instantly he was let inside. The chauffeur backed up the old-fashioned car and proceeded up Pine Street. Although Anne did not know it the car was a perfectly restored Duesenberg and was worth almost as much as the Quan Shang Laundry building.

After waiting for a few minutes Anne knocked. Blossom Wong herself stood next to the bouncer as he opened the door. Anne was surprised to see her dressed in an ivory colored Pèi with blue embroidery and smoking a cigarette in a long holder. In her right hand she held a brandy snifter, filled with brandy. Anne could hardly believe her eyes. No smoking or drinking were ever allowed in Blossom Wong's and now this?

"Don't be surprised," Blossom Wong said. "We all like to have a little fun once in a while.

This is Shanghai Night. You'll see." Blossom Wong extended her free hand and took Anne's. "Now, this way. You must put on something sexy." After a few steps Blossom Wong dropped her hand and stopped. "Well, I must get back to my friends. I'm sure you'll find yourself something."

Anne glanced into the parlor. The man who had arrived in the Duesenberg was walking toward Blossom Wong. "More lovely than ever," she heard him say. There were a few men clustered together. Probably telling saucy jokes, Anne thought. And there was a couple of Blossom Wong's girls that she barely knew, standing at the other end of the room and chatting among themselves. This hardly seemed like a party. Anyway, she was here. She may as well get changed and get cleaned up.

Over an hour had passed before Anne came out. She was a little nervous and had taken her time choosing a plum colored Qípáo, and trying to get her make-up just so. As she entered the parlor it seemed entirely transformed. For one thing, there were many more people. For another, some of them were white. And for another, many of them were smoking and drinking. Anne had never before seen white people in Blossom Wong's, and never smoking and drinking. But then, this was Shanghai Night. Anne hesitated not knowing where to stand in what was becoming a crowd. Thankfully, Blossom Wong stepped away from a small group that was listening intently to a Marine Major in dress blues.

"Here, I want you to meet a few people," Blossom Wong said as she took Anne's hand and guided her over to the group.

"I must say that you have chosen your Qípáo well. Plum colored. I would never have imagined, and the matching lipstick. I can even smell a trace of the Chanel #5 that I leave out for you girls, but very few of you use it. Well, here are my friends."

"Major Dan Kaljian. I want you to meet San San. She comes from Quangzhou."

"I've never had a chance to go there. Perhaps in my next tour," the major replied in a quiet but firm tone of voice.

Anne had read about the Marine Corps role in the Boxer Rebellion in school. This man did not seem as vicious as her schoolbook had portrayed the Marines. Thankfully times were different now.

A waiter dressed in a white dinner jacket approached with a tray of drinks. He extended the tray to Blossom Wong. "I'm afraid I've had my fill for now," she said. He turned to one of the white ladies. One of them took a martini, the other a ginger ale, and another like Blossom Wong, declined. Anne hesitated, not knowing which drink to reach for.

"Why not try the martini?" the marine suggested, reaching for a glass. Anne started to take it if from him feeling a little relieved that she did not have to make a choice.

"Thank you, Major," Blossom Wong said, smiling but with authority in her voice, "But San San much prefers the lemonade. Don't you dear."

"Well... yes. I always drink lemonade," Anne replied, not wishing to go against Blossom Wong in this or in any other matter.

"Lemonade, it is then," the major replied.

Everyone took a drink from the waiter's tray. The women who worked at Blossom Wong's, however, had lemonade. Although Blossom Wong had not said anything to them, they realized that what she had said to San San also applied to them.

Blossom Wong raised her glass.

"To a delightful Shanghai Night."

Everybody in the group raised their glass and clinked it against Blossom Wong's.

"To a delightful Shanghai Night," they said in unison.

"Now major continue where you left off just before San San arrived."

"I may have to backtrack a bit... we were on a night patrol in Vietnam. I was on the point, a little ahead of the platoon. Suddenly I get this gut feeling that someone is behind me and to my left. I always carried a knife unsheathed. I pretend to trip, purposely making a lot of noise,... let the bastard get overconfident..., then I whirl around. I see a dark form. I stab at chest level and hit my mark. Quickly I grab for his throat and stab again. As my men come by, I get them off the trail, then we open up on a Cong patrol coming up on our rear."

The major swirled the brandy in his snifter then took a sip.

"I've often wondered," he said thoughtfully. "One of my men ended up missing in action. What if that had been him? I had to act. I couldn't exactly give an interview."

Blossom Wong patted the major's sleeve.

"We all know, Major, that war can be clouded or black as night. I shudder to think about what happened to my sister during the Rape of Nanking. But enough of this gloomy talk, my friend Dr. Lewis Specker the dentist is going to have a dental plan for my girls."

"Why not," Dr. Specker said. "My accountant says 'yes', then, of course, I say 'yes'."

Anne could not believe her ears. A dental plan? She was hardly going to wear her teeth out chewing on penises. But then the whiter and brighter her smile and those of the other girls, the more money men would likely to fork over. And Blossom Wong would have more money still. Yes. Yes. It made sense.

As if reading her thoughts Blossom Wong took the long cigarette holder out of her mouth, smiled smugly, and threw her head back as if she were generosity itself.

"Now Dr. Specker," Blossom Wong said. "You really must explain to us how you got that awful scar on your right thigh."

Anne arched her eyebrows. The scar on his right thigh? How would Blossom Wong know about that? Did she have an affair with him just to bring the price of the dental plan down? Anne wouldn't put it past her. She looked around. Yan Yun seemed to be doing a good job of suppressing a laugh, though no one else seemed to let on that they were in the least bit surprised.

"Well," Dr. Specker began a bit uncomfortably, as if knowing that spicy thoughts had raced through minds though faces might not show it.

"When I was in the army in Germany I was racing in the Munich Six Day Bike Race, partnered with Hans Kreuger. We were doing pretty well until on the third night of the race when I swung up the banking on relief, some drunken German leaned over the railing, spilled beer on the track just in front of me, and down I slid in the boards. You've seen the results," he said turning to Blossom Wong.

"Now. Now, Doctor. I would hardly know how to administer to your leg. On the other hand, if you ever get bitten by a black widow I believe I could be of considerable assistance."

Whatever Blossom Wong meant by this Anne did not know but everyone threw their heads back and laughed as did Anne herself.

"And Captain Hebel," Blossom Wong said, obviously enjoying herself. "How are things in the police department?"

"As usual, but perhaps we ought to hear something from some of your girls."

"My girls are young. They haven't lived such interesting lives yet."

Blossom Wong said this in such a manner that she let it be known that she wanted her girls' lives to remain a mystery.

Their lives were interesting enough, Anne thought: sex and more steamy sex. Best to keep up appearances. By all means, keep up appearances.

"We had an incident a couple of weeks ago," Captain Hebel began. "A ship from Columbia came into Pier 80. Customs and the Coast Guard check 'em out but we get involved too sometimes. I'm way down the front of the dock near Third Street, with a pair of binoculars, where nobody can see me. As the Coast Guard and Customs are going up the gangway with their dogs, I see two crew members throw something off the opposite side.

"I look and I see three old tires bobbing in the bay. Eight hours later and the ship sails. Checked out clean as a whistle. I put a watch on the tires. Police dressed as homeless people, bikers, whatever. A week goes by. Now I'm taking heat from brass. Get the tires, check 'em out. No. Wait. We'll blow it, I argue. I'm given three more days. At dusk toward the end of the second day, two guys drive by in a pickup, the bed filled halfway with old tires. They stop, scratch their heads, break open a couple of cans of beer and start discussing. Suddenly one of them jumps in the bay, swims, the other throws him a rope. He ties it around the three tires and brings the end of the rope back to his friend. Soon he's back on the pier and they haul the tires up by tying the rope around the bumper and backing up the truck. As they're about to drive off my men, dressed as bikers and bums but armed with shotguns and more, converge on them. The tires were filled with cocaine. It was a big bust."

"My, my, Captain," Blossom Wong said approvingly. "You're always a jump ahead of these criminals, no wonder crime is down."

"No, I made a big mistake," Captain Hebel said quietly. "We should have followed them to wherever they were going. This way we only got two men but Tony Serra, a damn good lawyer, got them off. They claimed they were only junkmen and had no idea what was in the tires."

"Don't be so hard on yourself," the marine said sympathetically. "You certainly outthought the Coast Guard," he said in a condescending tone of voice.

"Now that we've all had a round of stories, Blossom Wong. How about yourself? I've heard that you once were an opera singer," the marine said.

"So I was," Blossom Wong said. "But I wasn't very good, so I had to train for another profession."

"Don't believe her," Dr. Specker said. "The only thing that stopped her was the communist takeover."

"Well, I did train under the famous tan Mei Lan-fang."

"See I told you," Dr. Specker said. "And I'll bet even now she could show us something."

"I have forgotten much, but there is one opera that was one of my favorites: 'The Faithful Concubine'. She was a beautiful woman much like San San here."

At this San San held her breath. She smiled, pretending to be amused, but she felt all eyes were on her.

"As I remember it, in the last scene," Blossom Wong went on. "The villainous groom could not resist the repeated offerings of wine by the bride so that he became hopelessly intoxicated. Then the loyal but avenging woman drew his sword and drove it through the breast of the ungrateful monster. It goes like this," Blossom Wong said as she demonstrated. "Here Major, down the hatch."

The major, a little surprised, gulped down the rest of the brandy.

"Now stumble and lie down."

The major did as he was told. It was obvious that getting drunk and falling down were nothing new to him.

Though no instructions had been given, the group formed a circle to give the major more room. Everyone in the parlor stopped talking and drinking.

Blossom Wong gracefully extended both of her arms, the long sleeves of her Pèi flowing as she did so. Accompanying her movements she began singing in a high falsetto voice. She looked down at the major. There was a mischievous smile on her face. She bent forward slightly, inspecting the major. Her head turned to the side, as if to see if anyone was watching. She bent down, kneeling on her right knee and extending her left leg back. Her right sleeve tipped toward the floor and her left sleeve extended upward. All these movements were smooth and flowed into each other. Then with a quick jerky motion Blossom Wong pretended to extract a sword from the major's "sheath." She arose holding the "sword", and pointed it down at the major. Her left hand was extended high above her. Her long flowing sleeves accented her pose. She looked down on him condescendingly, then bending her right knee and still holding her left hand high in the air with one quick motion she drove the "sword" into the major's ribs. She remained in this pose for a moment, then arose, spread her arms, covered by the flowing sleeves of the Pèi, bowed her head slightly, then ceased singing, and smiled at the audience as if she had just awakened from a dream. Everyone in the room began to clap. The mayor started to get up.

"Major Kaljian, wait please," Blossom Wong said. "San San also wishes to perform."

No, I can't, San San thought, looking at Blossom Wong with pleading eyes only to be met with steely eyes that said: You can and you must.

"Now stand over here where I am standing. Do as I did, though you need not slavishly imitate it."

Anne's heart pounded. Here she was on stage. The audience was waiting. As Blossom Wong began singing, Anne took a few mincing steps, stopped, looked at the major as if happy that he was passed out drunk. She went through the same movements as Blossom Wong, performing them as well as she could.

Though she liked the way her arms felt as she moved them in the way Blossom Wong had moved hers, she wished she were wearing a Pèi for the effect of flowing sleeves would be that much more dramatic. Finally the last few movements. She extended her left hand upward behind her and her right in front of her and down. She now thrust forward as if to stab the major, then she stepped back, stood up and brought her hands to her sides.

There was a muffled round of applause. For someone who had seen the performance only once Anne had done remarkably well.

The major started to get up again.

"Major Kaljian. Wait just a minute please," Blossom Wong said. "San San surprised me. I didn't realize she was such a natural performer, but her last few movements were not quite right. Listen to me San San. You must drive the sword in like you really mean it. You are the faithful concubine. You have been forced to marry this bastard against your will. You have gotten him drunk, and you will now avenge your lover."

Blossom Wong stepped away for a moment, then returned, holding a sword in both hands.

"Here my dear San San is a real sword from the Shang Dynasty. You will no longer have to imagine."

Anne gasped, as did everyone else. The sword was long with a very large, curved hilt and an ornate gold inlaid handle with the outline of a bird: a real museum piece. Anne doubted that there was any connection to her husband's great-grandfather's first name, still the name "Shang" which she saw on the sign in front of the laundry and which she said every day when answering the laundry phone grated on her ears, and that was not the only thing. Anne had seen the sword before in the Pang Fei Antique store. She wondered if the old scholar was trying to play some kind of joke on her. Anyway, there were too many coincidences. These must have happened for a reason. There must be some hidden truth.

Anne grasped the sword, which was quite heavy. Thank goodness she had worked in the laundry for her arms were very strong.

"Don't worry Major," Blossom Wong assured him. "San San will thrust the blade to the side of you."

Major Kaljian merely smiled although he knew San San would be acting. Even if she weren't, he had fended off worse in bayonet practice and in combat itself.

"Now remember what I told you San San," Blossom Wong reminded her, "This is your husband. You will now avenge your lover. Stab deep. Drive the blade home."

As Blossom Wong began to sing, Anne raised her left hand behind her, took a step forward, slowly lowered her sword, stopped, then quickly plunged it into her "husband's" chest, piercing his heart. The audience held its breath for she had just grazed the side of the major's dress blue shirt. San San slowly withdrew the sword inch by inch giving her hand a slight twist as she did so, then held the sword in front of her and put her left hand on her hip.

The room was silent. Someone yelled "Bravo," someone else yelled, "Still such a beautiful voice," then there was clapping, and more cheers rang out. "Bravo. Bravo."

"Well done. Well done," Blossom Wong said. "A little more realistic than is correct. But well done nonetheless, and with your willowy waist, you certainly outdid me. I will take the sword back now." Reluctantly Anne handed it over. She wished that Geary had been lying on the floor instead of the major and that she had buried the sword deep into his heart. Major Kaljian started to get up, holding his back as he did so. Blossom Wong grabbed hold of his hand, though he could certainly stand up without her help, and merely pretended to be assisted by her.

"Closer than I had expected. Actually, I had to move aside a fraction of an inch," he said with a laugh. "I'm usually not the one who's on the deck," the major said after he got up.

"Here, waiter. Give Major Kaljian a brandy to revive his spirits," Blossom Wong said. "Enough seriousness. I see the band is ready. I've tried to make it authentic... a little like Bunk Johnson's band used to be. You'll see."

Anne looked behind her. There in the corner of the room were five musicians. Three black and two white.

"Let's have some fun," Blossom Wong said. "Let's have some fun. "

The band started to play "The Radinsky March" with a really lively beat. Eight of Blossom Wong's girls led by Yan Yun entered from the hallway entrance. They had on short black skirts, narrow black suspenders, but were otherwise bare on top. They wore black pillbox hats at a jaunty angle, and black lace gloves complementing their fishnet stockings. Each had her right hand on the shoulder of the girl in front of her. They waved their free hands, saluted and took off their hats on every fourth count of the music while wiggling their bottoms in tune with the beat as they approached the area in front of the band.

"Les girls," Blossom Wong announced, "les girls."

Applause and whistles.

Yan Yun and the other girls now formed a chorus line in front of the band. High stepping, then breaking into a high-kicking chorus line. Several of the girls winked at the men.

Anne was surprised, though she should not have been, that "Les girls" had no underpants on. *They seem so sexy and filled with energy*, Anne thought. *Blossom Wong must have the most beautiful and sexy girls in all Chinatown.* Though Anne worked here too, she did not think of including herself.

The band stopped. Several of "Les girls" pursed their lips and blew kisses to the men. After a brief pause there was a drumbeat, and the band began playing "The Charleston." "Les girls" as Blossom Wong had called them immediately sprang to life with quick and lively steps, their breasts bouncing in time with the music.

Then they turned around, bent over, and wiggled their bottoms. They faced forward again, laughing as they danced. All too soon the band stopped.

"Les girls" now began mixing with the crowd. Anne heard one of them speaking to a gray-headed Caucasian man in French. *Now where did she learn French?* Anne asked herself. Anne had studied English in school, but perhaps she should have studied French too, it seemed so much more sophisticated. The major and the police captain were entertaining Blossom Wong with amusing antidotes. "It was a Navy bar, but we weren't about to be stopped," she heard the major say.

The trumpet player announced "Blue Skies." "Shall we, Major?" Anne heard Blossom Wong say as she handed the waiter her glass.

They cut a fine figure: Blossom Wong in her flowing Pèi, and the major in his dress blues. Anne felt a light tap on her shoulder. As she turned around, she recognized the man who had been chauffeured there in the Duesenberg. With his slicked back hair, double-breasted suit with wide lapels, and a diamond stickpin in his tie, he looked like a Chinese gangster in a 30's movie. He certainly was a good dancer, taking long gliding strides which she followed with ease. They turned, and whirled, then turned again. Finally, the music stopped. The man bowed slightly, then uttered his name in such a halting manner that Anne could not understand it. He was graceful on his feet, but he was now shy with a lovely stranger. Anne, too, made a slight bow, then the man disappeared into the crowd.

The band now played the soft and melodious sounds of "Summertime." The major was talking to a few of his friends. Anne brushed against his sleeve and said "Hello." He took the hint and asked her to dance. Although he had danced reasonably well with Blossom Wong, he definitely was not the dancer her previous partner had been. Anne pressed herself close to him, synchronizing her movements with his. She closed her eyes briefly, feeling his body and listening to the music. She opened them dreamily. What? There was Yan Yun and the police captain gliding by. Yan Yun still had on her cabaret outfit: a short black skirt with no underpants, black pill box hat, and topless except for her black suspenders. Yan Yun gave her a wink as if to say: I've caught the police captain and I am not about to let him go.

Anne clung to the marine. For now, she was his. Although he had danced reasonably well with Blossom Wong whenever he was at a little distance from her, he had two left feet; so they danced close, more like an embrace. She found herself guiding him. Soon they were down the hallway and had turned the corner. Here she was alone with a marine whose regimental forefathers had been the enemy during the Boxer Rebellion and here she was as if by instinct or intention going down on the enemy during Shanghai Night.

When they returned Blossom Wong looked at the major as if he had been naughty boy, but what else could be expected as boys will be boys, especially around enticing women.

Blossom Wong soon had a group of her intimate friends around her including the major. Anne listened, not always knowing why people roared with laughter. The waiter brought her a glass of ginger ale. Anne started to refuse, but Blossom Wong looked at her as if to say: Drink, wash your mouth out dear.

And so went the night with more entertaining conversation, more music and dancing. It was sexy and it was fun.

All too soon, although it was probably about 4 a.m., Blossom Wong was shaking the hands of her guests as they left. Anne, Yan Yun, and the other girls also shook their hands and smiled. As Blossom Wong was nearest to the door hers was the last hand they touched and the last face they saw.

There was laughter in the alleyway which faded until the door was shut.

"Girls. I have a little surprise for you," Blossom Wong said. "Most of the men gave me some money although I begged them not to. Here."

She laid the money out on the table. "It comes to about two hundred dollars apiece for each of you. I'll take the remainder of course," she said with a twinkle in her eye.

"Now tell me. Wasn't it fun? Wasn't it just like my Shanghai?"

She did not wait for an answer but went back to her room as if Shanghai Night would always be hers and would always be real.

32

The goldfish rippled through the water. It swam to the far end of the pond then vanished underneath the water lilies. Anne stuck her bare foot in the water. She circled it a couple of times before taking it her foot out. The Japanese Tea Garden in Golden Gate Park, Anne felt, would make her know the true essence of Japan and of Yoshi himself. She walked over the stone bridge pressing her heels into the slime and feeling it with her toes. A blackbird was perched on a Japanese maple. As she approached it flew off. She saw a beautiful red triangle on the front of each wing. Anne had never seen such a vivid contrast of red against black. Even her menstrual blood oozing out of her vagina and onto her black pubic hair was not like this. Anne put her shoes back on, walked up to the tea house and sat down underneath the verandah. A young Japanese woman in a pink kimono with white cranes embroidered on it and a red sash around her thin waist asked Anne in a soft voice. "Do you wish tea?"

Anne looked at a list of teas on the post of the verandah.

"What kind of tea do they prefer in Japan?"

"We often drink green tea."

"Yes, green tea, then."

The tea house hostess walked away with bold smooth steps. Soon she returned with a pot of tea, a light brown cup that was painted with a blue Japanese character, and a saucer with a fortune cookie.

"Three-twenty," the Japanese woman said graciously, Anne paid with a five. The waitress smiled and took the money but did not say anything in Japanese as Anne had hoped. Anne watched the goldfish in the pond. Two of them swam to the shade of a fern. A dragonfly flew in zigzag patterns. Was it catching insects or was that merely the way it flew? Anne wondered.

An elderly Japanese couple walked up the path and sat down on the opposite side of the tea house. Anne heard the hostess laugh at something they said. She strained to overhear them. Japanese seemed such a beautiful language and the waitress spoke it almost like a bird. So this was the competition: elegant, refined, and with a song-like voice. It was a wonder that Yoshi paid any attention to her.

Anne drank her tea. It was more bitter than she was used to. Was this the way they served tea in Japan? She had heard about the tea ceremony. She should learn more about it. She decided to leave some of her tea as if Yoshi were here and he wanted to share it with her. Eagerly she now broke open the fortune cookie. "You have a deep appreciation of the arts and music," the little slip of paper said. How true that was and how even sex was an art with its music. She thought about the red-winged blackbird. It had an art and a way, and the way pointed to Yoshi's heart.

33

Time passed, more slowly than she wished, until Anne saw Yoshi again, until the Lincoln Town car sped down Sutter Street toward the Hotel Kabuki.

It seemed an eternity until Anne heard the door latch click open. Yoshi was there. She could hear his receding footsteps. Anne paused, then let herself in. It was the same familiar room that Yoshi always took when staying at the Hotel Kabuki. She could hear him peeing in the toilet. She quickly began to undress. The red-winged blackbird in the Japanese Tea Garden had given her an idea. She had thought it through. She had thought every bit of it through. She would surprise Yoshi. She would catch him completely unaware.

Anne slipped out of her clothes. She let them fall on the floor. Yoshi was too fussy. A little untidiness would do him good. Anne pulled a pair of bright red socks out of her purse. After she had put them on, she stepped over to the mirror. She looked at her black lacquered nails as well as her black lipstick, which she had painted on that morning. With her raven hair and her bright red socks, she had transformed herself and she was now a bird of prey.

She was also the red-winged blackbird. Anne took red lipstick and quickly drew a red slash under her left armpit, and then under her right one.

Yoshi was startled when he walked out of the bathroom. He thought he had seen everything and now this. It was such a simple image: the red socks, the raven hair, the black lipstick, and black nails, like a living painting etched into his soul.

Anne felt the hard muscles of Yoshi's chest as she pushed against it with her hand. The muscles of a snake were more powerful than a bird. Yet a bird could overcome a snake, Anne reasoned. As Yoshi now lay on the bed Anne approached, strutting. With one hop she was on the bed, then devouring Yoshi's penis, now on it. She spread her arms. They were wings. A red-winged blackbird has power. A woman has more power. Yoshi looked at her red socks and her glistening black hair and the red slash marks underneath her armpits. Subtlely Anne's face changed. Her eyes became deeper and more penetrating, her nose sharper and more angular. Her lips pursed and her mouth was open as if ready to bite on something. She raised one arm slightly up, the other slightly down, as if catching thermals. Yoshi gazed up at the red slashes. He could feel her power. He could feel it pulsating between her legs. The thermals subsided. Anne needed to flap her wings to gain altitude. But how? Anne remembered Blossom Wong's sleeve movements with her Pèi. They were slow, majestic, fingers in a wide-open gesture. Now she moved the backs of her hands past Yoshi's face. He could see the red slashes underneath her black nails, talons. Anne moved them as she had seen Yan Yun do. Anne reached behind her with her left hand and with the tips of her sharp nails, very lightly scratched Yoshi's testicles as she rocked her pelvis. Yoshi's penis began to swell up even harder than it was. Anne withdrew her hand for a moment, then again lightly raked the tips of her nails against his testicles. Yoshi's whole body began to tremble. He had never felt such pleasure.

Yoshi looked at Anne's ink black hair and the red slashes underneath her armpits. Suddenly she reached forward with her right hand, extending her fingers. Was she going to caress his face? She gripped his throat lightly then began tightening her grip, sinking in her nails. Yoshi kept ejaculating. The death grip had accelerated his flow. Finally, Anne opened her hand and kissed him with her black lips. The bird had overcome the snake which now lay limp in the grass.

Yoshi awoke gasping for air. He looked around. The room was empty. Was last night a dream? Or a nightmare? He quickly ran into the bathroom. He looked at his neck. There were five small red marks on it, from which tiny drops of blood flowed. Last night was real. He had been attacked by a red-winged blackbird and he had enjoyed every minute of it.

34

Yoshi felt the soft hand of the Japan Airlines stewardess on his shoulder. "Are you all right?" she asked. "You shouted something in your sleep, and you are sweating. Perhaps, you have a fever." Yoshi felt his forehead. Yes, it was damp with sweat. "I'm all right. I was dreaming there were terrorists aboard." He said not wanting to tell the truth. "We take serious precautions," the stewardess reassured him. "If you need anything…"

After the stewardess left Yoshi thought about his dream as it really was. A bird with a bright red mark on each wing had attacked him, pecking at his neck. He had fought it off, but to no avail. Then the bird had transformed itself into a woman. Yes, her, with her bright red socks, ink black hair, red slashes underneath her armpits, black lips and nails. Those talons had ripped at his neck, and that is when the stewardess woke him. Would he have lived if she had not intervened, he wondered? People died in their sleep. Maybe their dreams suffocated them.

Yoshi looked at this watch. In two hours, the plane would land. Soon he would see his wife and daughter and attend to his business.

35

Yoshi looked over at his daughter. She had hardly touched her food. She hadn't eaten her rice at all and had taken just a few bites of her eel.

"Not hungry tonight?" Yoshi asked.

"I don't like American rice, and I don't like eel," his daughter answered, turning up her nose.

"The Americans send us only the best quality rice. Blindfolded you would say so."

"I can't eat Daddy. I can't eat American rice. And I don't like eel. Ugh. Please Daddy may I be excused?"

Yoshi turned to his wife.

"Let her leave," she said.

"Yes, if you are not hungry. Certainly, you may leave."

"Thank you."

His daughter got up, smiled at both of them, started taking quick steps toward her room.

"I'm sure it's not the food," Yoshi said, turning toward his wife. "She doesn't see me very often, probably she's just upset."

"I wish that were the reason," his wife replied. "But many nights it is the same. She just picks at her food or takes a few bites. And sometimes she doesn't come home until late."

"How late?" Yoshi asked.

"Eight o'clock. Sometimes nine."

"How often?"

"Once, maybe twice a week."

"Is this the truth?" Yoshi asked.

"Yes," his wife replied. "But it is not as bad as all that. Her grades are still near the top of her class. She studies late. I can see the light on in her room."

Yoshi smiled. He certainly was relieved to hear that.

"She has your drive you know," his wife added.

"Don't be humble. You were the one who was first or nearly first in every class. Yes, even in math and physics."

His wife blushed.

"My drive came later when I realized I had to make a living. I played too much baseball when I was young."

"And she plays too much tennis," Yoshi's wife said smiling. "Though how she maintains her figure I don't know. You'd think she'd be a beanpole as little as she eats."

"Well," Yoshi said, "Part of the problem is that I haven't been around much."

"You work so hard."

"Too hard. Sometimes I work so hard that I don't think clearly. At work I often make bad decisions."

"Well, you certainly make a good salary."

"A little less and we could live just as well."

Yoshi looked at his daughter's uneaten rice and eel.

"Perhaps, I better see her. We haven't had a talk in a while... over a year. I won't be long."

Yoshi knocked on his daughter's door.

"May I come in?" he asked.

"No," she said sharply.

Such lack of respect, he thought. *I would never have spoken that way to my parents or any of my elders.*

Yoshi started to step away, then stopped. Why shouldn't he see his daughter in her room? He was her father. He owned the house. He paid the bills. Abruptly, Yoshi turned the handle and pushed open the door.

His daughter was sitting in front of her desk. A book was next to her, and she was typing on the computer.

"I'm doing my homework Daddy," his daughter said without looking up. Yoshi looked around the room. There was a Coco Chanel purse hanging from her chair. The closet was open. He could see racks of clothes. Although he couldn't exactly tell from a distance, they all looked like clothes a high fashion model might wear; and they were all obviously expensive. Wait, that was not the Toshiba computer he bought her. No, it was a Macintosh from America. Where did she get the money? Yes, he gave her a reasonable allowance, but it was not enough to buy these things. No not by a longshot.

Suddenly it hit him. It was too obvious. His wife had said, "I don't know why she's not as skinny as a beanpole, the way she eats." His daughter had a trim athletic figure. She played tennis hard. She was not hungry, and she was getting money from someplace. She must be going out on money compensated dates with older men. Yoshi had read about this in the newspaper. Older rich men took pretty teenage high school girls out to restaurants or shopping or simply gave them money to go out with them. Sometimes they had sex, but oftentimes they did not. The older man had a date with a sexy-looking girl who otherwise would never have given him the time of day, and the girl now had expensive clothes or the money to buy an outfit to make the other girls envious. And his daughter was doing this. It was obvious.

"Do you have sex with them?" Yoshi asked.

"Daddy!"

"That part I do not want to know about," Yoshi said emphatically.

"But it is clear that you are having money compensated dates with rich older men."

His daughter hung her head.

"I know I am partly at fault. I have taught you money matters more than everything. I was wrong. I have hardly seen you or your mother in over a year. Business. Business. It has always been business."

His daughter started to cry. Yoshi put his hand on her shoulder. "I know there is a lot of competition from the other girls at school. But this is not the way."

"Please, Daddy, don't tell Mom."

"No, but please come home earlier and have dinner with her. Soon you will be in college, and she will not see you very much."

"I'll try Daddy. Please don't tell her."

"Of course not. Listen some of these old geezers will not be easy to break off with but do so."

Tears ran down his daughter's cheeks. Yoshi held her.

"I understand. I understand. But no matter what happens promise me you will see your mother more often."

"I promise."

Yoshi left the room. He had to admit to himself that even he was under his daughter's spell. She had learned well how to manipulate older men and she had learned it from him.

36

Yoshi heard his wife's voice as he entered the bedroom.

"Come in. You still like to go to bed with your wife, don't you?"

"Of course, but I want to go into the living room first. I think I left something there."

"I'll be ready for you."

Yoshi walked into the living room. There it was, his uncle's camphor wood chest. It looked almost new for the maid had kept it well polished. It was eighty years old, maybe older, not really that old for an heirloom. His uncle Seiji Yamoto had given it to him. "Here, take my war memories," he had said.

Yoshi remembered his uncle, a jovial thick-set man with a heavy jaw. One day he was alone with his uncle. He was studying, his books were laid out on the kitchen table, and he was eagerly reading his history book.

"Well, well. What's this?" his uncle said. "A young scholar already. My, I'm pleased." His uncle reached over and browsed through his history book.

"Lies. Lies. All lies."

"No Uncle, it is our history book."

"Yes, and not one word about Japanese atrocities during World War II."

"Atrocities?"

"Yes. Atrocities. Have you ever heard of the Bataan Death March? or Bilibid Concentration Camp? or the Rape of Nanking?"

"A little Uncle. But the teacher said there have been many American lies and untruths."

"Let me tell you real history, not some fancy fairy tale. I saw babies thrown in the air and caught on Japanese swords for sport. And rapes of innocent Filipino women and prisoners beaten to death for a trifle, and more."

"Uncle, be more respectful."

Yoshi's uncle suddenly gave him a quick sharp blow to the temple.

"Listen to me," his uncle shouted. "You show more respect. I was there, I know. I did some of these things myself."

Yoshi looked at this uncle in disbelief.

"Yes, it is true. And I am ashamed."

His uncle put his hand on Yoshi's shoulder.

"I want you to help build a new Japan. Our honorable traditions broke down during the war. For that I am sorry. But lies about our past won't help. Promise me to help build a new enlightened Japan."

"I promise Uncle," Yoshi said.

Tears started to run down his cheeks. Yoshi's uncle held his shoulder. He did not say,

"Japanese boys don't cry." "When I die, I will leave you a chest with some of my military things. It will remind you of me and of our conversation."

His uncle had died a few years later. Soon afterwards the chest was put in his room. Later, when Yoshi was grown and had bought a house of his own, he had it placed in the living room.

He had always kept the chest locked and the key with his personal keys. Whenever there was a crisis in his life, such as the time when he was still living with his parents and was having trouble with advanced algebra, Yoshi opened the chest and looked at his uncle's war memorabilia. This gave him comfort. This gave him strength.

Yoshi opened the chest slowly, reverently.

"What say you now Uncle? My firm is in trouble. And my daughter… Well, she could use better sense. And as for me, although I cannot make up for the rape of Nanking, I have treated Chinese women well." Yoshi touched some of the contents: his uncle's old uniform and sword. He looked at a faded photo of his uncle with some of his army comrades. There was a jungle in the background. Where was it taken? he had often wondered. There were even several pairs of his uncle's army socks and his underwear. Thank God his uncle had had everything cleaned before packing them away. What's this beneath the underwear? He felt cold steel. He ran his fingers along the barrel of a Marine Corps .45 pistol with a full clip of ammunition next to it.

What was the story behind it? Yoshi closed the trunk slowly. As always, he felt new strength.

"You certainly took long enough," Yoshi's wife said impatiently.

"I was thinking."

"About me? Or about business?"

"About business."

"I thought so. Well, maybe I can divert you."

Yoshi's wife began to undress. Carefully folding her clothes. Putting them away in the chest of drawers or hanging them up. Yoshi did likewise.

"Still thinking about business?" Yoshi's wife said looking at his flaccid penis. "I'll get your attention." She began to get down on her knees.

"No, no," Yoshi said. "I need something else."

Something else. What else was there? Except? "Viagra?"

"No. I need to kiss the Rising Sun. That will make me hard."

Kiss the Rising Sun? That will make him hard? She knew that Yoshi was patriotic, but this was sick. But if it would help, it would help.

"I think I have a small flag."

"No, I need to kiss the Rising Sun on your breasts."

"I could press it against my breasts."

"That is not what I mean," Yoshi said. "Do you have any red lipstick?"

"Of course."

"And something white. A liquid or a paste?"

"Just my white-out."

"Get them," Yoshi said.

Yoshi's wife went to her dresser and her desk. She brought back the lipstick and the white-out, feeling like a little girl bringing something to her kindergarten teacher. What was going on?

"Now hold still."

Yoshi began to apply red lipstick to each of her nipples. He then opened the white-out. Yoshi's wife cringed as he painted it on.

"Finished," he said at last. "It will dry shortly. There, look in the mirror." He led her over to the dresser.

Yoshi's wife looked at herself. She looked like some patriotic stripper in a low-class bar. What would her parents think? What would her daughter think? Or her friends? Did it matter?

"It must be dry by now," Yoshi said. He began kissing her nipples, kissing the Rising Sun. She could feel him getting hard and yet harder as she grabbed his penis. She had never felt him this hard before, even when they were young.

Now they were on the bed. She could feel every bit of his penis inside of her, thrusting gently, then harder, changing rhythms. He kept kissing her nipples while she came and came again. Then finally as if he had waited for her the whole time, she could feel his semen gushing out. Why was he turned on this way? If this was the spark their marriage lacked, perhaps they should do this more often.

Yoshi's wife kept her eyes closed. She wanted to remember this night, to savor it. She started laughing. If anyone knew. But they would not know. It was their secret and she had enjoyed it.

37

Yoshi sat in his office going over his presentation. Occasionally images of his wife's breasts with the Rising Sun painted on them flashed before his mind. He must concentrate on his work he told himself. The charts were already in the conference room. He looked over his speech one more time. He was as ready as he was every going to be.

As he walked into the conference room and toward the lectern all the Okamoto Electronics Firm employees rose. Even Mr. Hakamada pushed himself up with his cane. Although Yoshi did not demand this protocol, especially from old Mr. Hakamada whom Yoshi had often told that he need not stand in Yoshi's presence, it was accorded him nonetheless.

"Kindly be seated," Yoshi said.

Yoshi looked out over the rows of Okamato Electronics employees. There was Mrs. Obata sitting there rather stiffly for her young age, he thought. Some of the young tigers were in the front row. One, Mr. Yamaguchi looked like he'd had a few too many the night before. The young tigers had a way of acting that made him think they exchanged girlfriends, though this was probably not so. Mrs. Hagawa was seated behind them. She appeared uncomfortable, as if she wished she were seated someplace else, especially when one of them whispered something to another. Then there was his secretary with her notepad. She would carry it and write down what was said even if a parrot were on stage. Then there was Mr. Hakamada sitting off to the right of the front row. He had even placed an arrangement of ikebana flowers on the low platform of the stage just in front of him.

Yoshi began with a history of the firm. "Honorable Okamoto employees, some years ago I took over the failing Takaschima Electronics firm and renamed it after myself." There was slight laughter. Mrs. Obata covered her mouth with her hand. The young tigers stuck out their chests. A couple of them tugged at their ties, as if to say: yes, that is the way a man should act.

"At first earnings were rather low and in fact even lower than that of Takaschima Electronics, but then we kept expanding and hiring new people with drive and fresh minds." The young tigers looked at each other, congratulating themselves. Yoshi picked up a pointing stick and pointed at the chart mounted on a heavy easel with a thick plywood backing which showed the years on the horizontal axis and Yen on the vertical axis. There was a drastic dip after the year of the takeover, followed by a level line, "Gradually our policies of expansion and innovation began to catch on." Yoshi now pointed to an upswing in the line. The young tigers smiled. "And as you can see," Yoshi continued, "we have been going uphill ever since, though a little unevenly at times." Yoshi glanced at his audience who seemed totally captivated except for Mr. Hakamada who was still staring at his ikebana flower arrangement.

"Lately we have broken off our Asian markets and have been marketing exclusively in Germany with much of our research being done in America." Broad smiles broke out across the faces of the young tigers. "Yes. Germany. Japan's ally during World War II. A reliable market. A punctual people. Gorgeous women. Good sex shows. Yes. Germany."

"But as some of you know, during Hurricane Blanc all of our containers were lost at sea; and so our curve has taken a downturn," Yoshi pointed to a dip, "in profits." Yoshi flipped the chart over the back of the easel. Yoshi now stood next to a drawing made by Mrs. Obata. The drawing was of a German businessman with a large belly, an expanded vest covered it. He was smoking a cigar, and standing next to a diminutive Japanese businessman who wore a plain suit. Over the German businessman was a caption: "Your profits are for me." Yoshi now made a dramatic display of ripping the drawing off the easel.

There were a few gasps because this was totally unexpected and because the drawing while derogatory to the German, was quite good and it seemed a shame to see it torn off and tossed on the floor. Underneath, however, was another drawing which Mrs. Obata had made. Only in this drawing the Japanese businessman was taller, the German businessman smaller. Next to the Japanese businessman was a Japanese naval officer. The caption read: Japanese shipping the best there is. And underneath, another caption: Japanese corporate profits are for Japan. Yoshi looked at the Japanese in the drawing. He looked a little like Yoshi, and the naval officer a little like Mr. Hakamada. And the German businessman, a little like the office photo of Dr. Hans Schoeb. Although Yoshi had given Mrs. Obata some general ideas for the sketches, he had said nothing this specific. It was however, only natural though that she should draw the sketches this way. Yoshi looked down at his audience, which now sat there silently, anticipating. Mr. Hakamada looked straight ahead at his flower arrangement. The young tigers looked up, almost as if Yoshi were a tribal chief.

"It is time," Yoshi began, "to turn the corner. To start making profits again. Even if we have to kill our German markets and start anew with American ones. I have given some thought to this." With that Yoshi pulled out his uncle's .45 from his pocket and pointed it at the sketch of Dr. Hans Schoeb. "Even if Okamoto Electronics were to shoot the German with this American pistol." A few employees smiled, thinking it was a toy pistol.

Yoshi pointed the .45 at the sketch of the German. "Talk about drama," he heard one of the young tigers say. As Yoshi aimed the .45 at the sketch of Dr. Schoeb he thought to himself: *Why him? Why not aim at the sketch of the Japanese naval officer slightly to the left. Who would know the difference?*

Yoshi studied his audience. The young tigers were on the edge of their seats, Mrs. Obata sat there proudly, and Mr. Hakamada continued to look up at his Ikebana flower arrangement. *His flower arrangement. Always something from Japan's past,* Yoshi thought, *as if by remaining fixated in it the present would fade away.*

Damn, there was a problem right now. Yoshi had done some checking himself, and he saw no reason why Mr. Hakamada did not know that forty-eight containers could not be stowed underdeck or that the Get Clout.com Insurance Company was a sham. Hell, Mr. Hakamada was the culprit, not his sketch. Yoshi spun around, pointed the .45 at Mr. Hakamada, and pulled the trigger. One shot, two shots, three shots. Mr. Hakamada slumped forward; blood ran on the floor. Several people screamed. Mrs. Obata fainted in her chair. Most employees sat there in disbelief. Was this real? But no one was more stunned than Yoshi himself. He knew the gun was loaded, yet he had pulled the trigger. One of the young tigers said cynically, "Yes, that's it. Get rid of the old duffer. That's the spirit."

Yoshi froze. What had he done? What would his uncle think if he were alive? Or his wife? He thought of her, of kissing the Rising Sun on her breasts. He thought of his daughter with her Coco Chanel purse, and her money compensated dates with rich older men. He thought of the Chinese girl, his dream mistress. He thought of the characters written on her tummy that night, of her red socks, and black nails, and of the red dragon. He thought of his firm. There was no working capital. Who was he kidding? It was not coming back. The graphs. The sketches. They were all meaningless.

What was it like? What was death like? He didn't want to know, but he had no choice. He turned the pistol toward himself. He looked down the muzzle, then put it to his forehead. Bang. It was over. It was finished.

The young tigers sat there in disbelief. Their world was gone. It had happened so fast and been so unexpected that some people sat there, as if expecting the presentation to continue. But this was the final act, and it was over.

38

Anne watched as Mrs. Teng scrubbed a pair of men's Levi's in the sink. She could see Mrs. Teng's arm muscles flex and relax. She knew Mrs. Teng was all woman yet she was surprised that Mrs. Teng's arms looked so strong. Anne saw no reason why Mrs. Teng should work so hard at her age.

"You can run them through the washer as many times as you like. After the first time, the rest is on me," Anne said.

"There's piss in these pants. An old man in the apartment can no longer control himself."

"Still you can run them through."

"I'd rather scrub," Mrs. Teng said sharply.

"Anyway, I am sorry that the old man cannot control himself," Anne said.

"Why?"

"It must be hard on him."

"What if it is?" Mrs. Teng replied. "It is also hard on me. And besides he brought it on himself."

"Wouldn't it be old age that makes him incontinent?"

"No, he brought it on himself. By not fucking enough."

"Mrs. Teng, please."

"Listen. And I don't care who hears. When a man builds up too much semen, he can't pee and later he becomes incontinent and impotent. He's too selfish. He keeps it to himself."

"Mrs. Teng, we are in America. You must have medical evidence."

"I have. Every woman knows I speak the truth."

An older woman dressed in a faded black coat and baggy pants spoke up. "She is right. My husband is that way. And he is always selfish with money too."

A couple of other older women smiled as if in agreement. Anne looked at the women, wondering if they would want sex at their age.

"Don't underestimate us," Mrs. Teng said. "Don't ever underestimate us. We still yearn for a hot cock between our legs; and yes, in the mouth too."

Anne was certainly not going to argue. What did she know of their lives?

The phone rang. Anne tried not to hurry, yet she walked with quick steps. *Yoshi,* she thought, *The chauffeur is calling to say Yoshi is here.*

The chauffeur spoke more briskly than usual. "I'm parked near the alleyway on Stockton Street. Please meet me quickly."

"I'll be right there."

As Anne put down the receiver, she could see Mrs. Teng and several of the other women smiling at her. They knew the truth. She was the laundress, married, and had a lover. She immediately stepped out into Stark Alley. Anne could feel her chest heaving as she approached Stockton Street. There he was, sitting in the front seat of the Lincoln Town Car. She opened the door and climbed in the back seat. The chauffeur had no sooner driven a couple of blocks, than he slowly pulled over and parked in front of the Tong Fat Hotel. Was this some kind of joke? Anne thought. Yoshi would never meet in a place like this.

"Engine problems?" Anne asked after they had been there a few minutes.

"I wish to say something, miss."

"Well?"

"Yoshi is dead."

Anne sat there frozen. Was she hearing correctly?

The chauffeur repeated, "Yoshi is dead."

Tears started to roll down Anne's cheeks. This must be a dream. This must not be real.

"Yoshi's firm was facing bankruptcy, miss. He did not want to disgrace himself. He committed suicide."

Anne knew that these words were meant to soothe her and they did. Yes, how like Yoshi. She had felt it in his body. Pride and power. Power even to turn on himself.

"All I have is this town car, miss. It was registered in my name. This for years of service."

His service was minimal, Anne thought, driving Yoshi around on the few occasions he was in town, and acting as his interpreter. The chauffeur obviously had other more sinister employment. The town car plus his part-time wages were not a bad bargain.

"Only a car. It is very unfair miss. It is very unfair," the chauffeur repeated.

Here she was losing a lover, a sexual soulmate. The only person who had given her life meaning. How could he think of such a trifling matter at a time like this? How could he?

"Your husband, miss. He owns the laundry."

"Yes, he inherited it," Anne replied, wiping away her tears.

"And you do not like him."

"We don't get along."

The chauffeur started to laugh, stopped, then began in a serious tone. "Tomorrow miss. Tomorrow I will kill your husband at work. I will make it look like an accident. You will own the laundry building, outright. You will sell it and we will split: eighty percent for me and twenty percent for you. Your building is worth a million dollars."

Anne could not believe what she was hearing; yet she knew that the chauffeur meant every word he said. And the building...worth one million dollars? She had never known that. They were always skimping. But as she thought about it the only profits were from a few rent-controlled apartments, plus running the laundry, Geary's job plus what she earned at Blossom Wong's which probably went toward Geary's drinking, gambling, and whoring. And then there was the overhead: a large water bill and building repairs which were always high. They were property rich, yet they were just making it.

"Tomorrow night miss I will come by after you have closed. You will have the deed to your house. If you cannot find it, I will help you, then I will contact a real estate agent I know."

Anne's head was reeling. First Yoshi was dead. Now this.

"You will do as I say miss. Please go now."

Anne sat there for a second, then quickly opened the door. She wanted to get away. She wanted to get away fast. Anne slammed the door and quickly ran down the street.

39

At first Anne started to go back into the laundry, but then thought better of it, the customers would wonder why she returned so soon. They would gossip. No, she would go home. She would cook for Geary, and they would be together for the last time.

As she entered the apartment, she looked at it with different eyes. Though they did not have much furniture, there was a certain simplicity, a certain plainness that she really liked. There were not many rooms, but each room was reasonably spacious and while at first she had not liked the location, now she thought of it as quite ideal. It was in the heart of Chinatown which she had grown to love, because of the stores, the markets, and the chatter. Also because it was at the end of the alley, it was quiet.

Now, soon the building would be sold and her $200,000 would probably be reduced to $100,000 after taxes. That would not be nearly enough for a down payment on a house in San Francisco or most places in the Bay Area, and even if it were, she would have to take another job in a laundry and the salary would make any real estate agent laugh. She would have to rent, and a landlord would have total control of her life.

Anne decided to cook chow fun, one of Geary's favorite meals. As she stirred the noodles she tried to visualize Geary, but she could only see parts of him, his strong but rough hands, his disheveled hair, and yes, his stubby penis. She could not put the fragments together into one image as if she blocked him out, even though he did go to work every day, provided her with a nice apartment, although he did take much of her money from Blossom Wong's. She had seen the bills. It seemed like they were always catching up.

Anne could hear the unmistakable sound of Geary's Chevy pickup. Normally it irritated her, now she was only too glad to hear it. The engine stopped. It seemed like only a few seconds later when Geary opened the door, banging it against the doorstop. As usual he paid no attention to her but hurried to the bedroom to take off his work clothes. Soon she heard water running in the tub. Anne turned the gas on the stove as low as she could before she walked down the hallway to the bathroom.

Geary sat in the tub rubbing a bar of soap on a washrag. How like a little boy he looked, she thought, with his pudgy body and uncombed hair.

"Let me help you," Anne said as she gently took the wash rag from his hands and began scrubbing his back. Even through the wash rag it felt strong, quite unlike his pot belly. And so did his shoulders and arms as she now washed them. He certainly did not have the tapered defined physique of Yoshi or Ling Chiao, but what muscles he did have were from honest labor. Even though it made no difference now, still she wished he had a body like Yoshi. If Geary felt any pleasure in his wife's washing him, he gave no sign of it, but simply sat there as if he were a pack animal being taken care of until the next load.

Anne reached for a small plastic bucket that she sometimes used. She dipped it in the water and poured it on Geary's back. She could tell by the smile on his face that he really liked this. She dipped it in over and over, pouring very slowly.

"You're a good wife," Geary said.

Anne was so taken aback when Geary said this that she almost dropped the bucket. A good wife? She, who so afraid of the chauffeur that she would not tell her husband he was about to be murdered. She, who had an affair that had consumed every bit of her love.

"Geary, I have to get back to the kitchen," Anne replied worried that he might say something else in praise of her.

Anne put the chow fun on the table along with two bowls of rice and two cups of tea. Shortly Geary came in, dressed in his bathrobe, its belt cinched just beneath his belly. Without saying a word, he sat down, picked up his chopsticks and began to eat. After a while he looked over at her.

"Just eating a bowl of rice, and drinking tea?"

"I'm not hungry, Geary."

"Well then, more chow fun for me." He said this almost like a happy little boy.

Anne picked at her rice as Geary inhaled the chow fun. She had always thought him crude when he ate. But if he wanted to eat this way, what of it? Why not indulge him this simple pleasure after work. Geary leaned back and swallowed his tea.

"Good chow fun," Geary said. "Almost like my mother's."

"Not quite," Anne reassured him. "Look Geary," Anne said as she got up to do the dishes, "you needn't get dressed and help me clean and close up the laundry. Stay here. Relax. You push yourself too hard."

"Just tonight," Geary answered.

Geary got up and went into the bedroom while Anne finished the dishes.

That night there wasn't much to do in the laundry other than the routine chores of wiping off the washers and dryers, cleaning the floor, and counting the money. Anne was soon back in the apartment. As she opened the door to their bedroom she saw Geary in bed, his back against the headboard, holding a BMW auto repair manual. His head was bent forward, and he was fast asleep. Geary mumbled something, then eased himself onto his back as Anne took the book from his hands.

After Anne had undressed, she turned off the lights and slipped under the covers. She lay there on her back staring into the blackness. Yoshi was dead, his warm smile and groping hands, gone. She squeezed her thighs together, trying to remember him. Nothing. Like it or not Yoshi's penis and his tongue were dead. She reached for Geary's penis. Tickling it, then sought it with her mouth. She began sucking on it, not as she would have sucked on Yoshi's or a customer at Blossom Wong's, but as she would have sucked on her mother's nipple. Anne stopped. No, not yet. She threw back the covers. She sat on Geary's penis, down slowly, then rocking back and forth. Geary cupped her breasts. She hesitated, pressed herself against him, pushing down hard against his penis. As she could feel him climax, she whispered in his ear, "Geary I love you." Anne lay on top of Geary for a few moments, not daring to move. She wanted to look into his eyes, but they were enveloped in the darkness. The minutes went by, soon Anne could hear Geary snoring. She pushed herself off him and snuggled up to his side. "I love you Geary," she said. But she could not bring herself to warn him about tomorrow. Were these then hollow words? And was she not now really a prostitute?

40

Anne awoke with a start. She reached over. Geary was gone. "Geary," she called out. His name echoed against the walls. There was no response but her own, calling his name again. Anne quickly dressed and hurried over to the laundry. She unlocked the door and turned on the lights, but she did not stay. She did not want to see any customers or to hear their gossip and complaints, not today. No sooner had Anne returned and sat back down on Geary's chair in the kitchen than the telephone rang. She picked it up anticipating the worst, but hoping it was Geary and everything was all right.

"Hello, Anne, this is Yuan. Your husband met with an accident," he said hesitantly. "Somehow he made a mistake with the rack and it came down on him. The police are here. I found him dead when I came in."

Anne started to cry. "Are you sure?" she asked.

"Yes. Yes. He was such a good mechanic."

Anne hung up the phone. *He made a mistake with the rack,* she thought. *Sounds like Yuan's afraid of a lawsuit.* Well, he needn't worry. She knew the truth. Or about how it went. Geary went in early as usual. The chauffeur knocked him out with some kind of martial arts punch, then lowered the rack on him. Later Yuan came in and found him dead.

Anne's head felt light. Tears trickled down her cheeks. She fell asleep where she was, drifting into a dream. Geary was caressing her breasts. He was a younger man with a softer touch, much like Yoshi's. She was sitting on his lap, feeling his penis inside of her. Yoshi entered the room dressed in his business suit. Geary and Anne stood up. Yoshi looked at their naked bodies and they looked at him. They remained like that, then slowly faded.

When Anne awoke, she did not know how much time had passed though she could tell by the way the sunlight and the shadows mixed in the alleyway that it must have been a few hours.

She rubbed her eyes. Tea would wake her up, Anne thought. As she started to boil the water, the phone rang. Anne's hand shook as she picked up the receiver.

"This is the coroner's office. Is this Mrs. Anne Quan?"

"Yes."

"Your husband Geary Quan was killed accidentally when a car rack came down on him. His employer gave us your phone number and his name, and we have also identified him through his fingerprints. In a day or so you should tell us what funeral arrangements you want to make and the phone number of the funeral parlor. Our address is 850 Bryant Street, and the phone number is 865-0700. You need not come down here as positive identification has been made."

"Thank you," Anne answered.

Well, the chauffeur had certainly done a professional job. She was not surprised. Funeral arrangements? They had passed the Chinese Cemetery in South San Francisco on the way to the Serramonte Shopping Center. Geary had said that his father and grandfather were buried there. She assumed that he had wanted to be buried there too. Tomorrow she would look the number up in the phone book.

The tea was ready. Anne poured it, savoring the aroma. The hot tea warmed her hands as she sat there holding the cup. Geary was dead. The coroner had determined that. But was Yoshi dead? Anne had only the chauffeur's word. Why not phone Japan? Why not find out for sure? She certainly need not worry about Geary seeing the phone bill.

She reached into her purse for her copy of Yoshi's business card. There it was on the bottom underneath an old comb she never used. It was folded over four times though she could think of no particular reason why she had done this. Anne unfolded her copy of the card. Yes, there was Yoshi's business phone number. Anne immediately proceeded to dial the number without even considering what time it was in Japan.

She heard a female Japanese voice speaking in Japanese. She was afraid of this, but thankfully shortly later what sounded like the same voice spoke in Cantonese, "This is Okamoto Electronics, please hold, a message will follow in Japanese, Cantonese, English and German." After a short pause the message in Japanese began. Anne listened intently though she could not understand it. How delightful it was to hear Japanese. It sounded so elegant, so refined. She only wished it were Yoshi's voice. The message finished then another began in Cantonese. "We are sad to inform you that due to financial reasons Okamoto Electronics is no longer in business. Also, most unfortunately Mr. Okamoto met with an untimely death on April

10th. To all our loyal customers we express our deepest regrets." The message began again only this time in English. Anne hung up the phone. She did not want to hear of Yoshi's death again.

So it was definitely true. Yoshi was dead, and it had now been two weeks. Anne thought back. Two weeks ago? Could anything have happened then that was an omen? The only thing that she could think of was that two weeks ago while she was walking down Stockton Street, she felt something crawling on her cheek. She thought it was a mosquito and slapped it with her hand. It turned out to be a ladybug. Anne felt sad that she had killed it. Was it Yoshi saying farewell? Had he died at that moment? She was not superstitious, but she felt that this was so, and that Yoshi forgave her for killing the ladybug.

Anne sipped her tea. She looked at the leaves, hoping they would respond to her thoughts. The chauffeur had said that it was unfair... that the only thing that he had for his years of service was a Lincoln Town Car. But his service was a few days out of every two or three months of the year at most. It was obvious that he was some kind of underworld character and that he received extra money and the use of the car from Yoshi. And since Yoshi's death the car was his. What was unfair about that? Now he wanted her to sell the laundry building, keep $800,000 for himself and give her $200,000. And his share would be cash, she could be sure of that. Plus, she would have to pay taxes on the entire amount. She had not really thought of this before. Who knew what other financial schemes he might have up his sleeve? It was definitely unfair. Yoshi, she felt, would never have stood for this sort of a business deal. Why then should she? And besides he would have wanted her better taken care of than this. She should listen to his spirit. She had been Yoshi's lover. She had sucked his penis and had felt his semen come hot on her mouth and in her vagina. The chauffeur had been Yoshi's part-time employee. There was no way he should usurp her. She slowly finished her tea and went over in her mind what she should do. Finally, it dawned on her. There was something she could do, and now that she had thought about it, she was determined to do it.

41

Smoke drifted out of the open door of The Buddy Bolen Jazz Club on Fillmore Street. Supposedly the police cited smokers, but unlike the other bars and restaurants along Fillmore Street there were no anxious people outside smoking nervously until they could go back in. Anne walked in and sat down at the bar. At the far end of the bar was a heavyset ruddy-faced cop laughing and joking with a black prostitute who took her cigarette out of her mouth and threw her head back whenever she laughed at something he had said. There were several seedy-looking characters seated at the bar. One with a scar on his right cheek and a broken nose looked like an ex-prize fighter. The few women in the bar looked like prostitutes resting their legs in between shifts. None of the men was paying any attention to them as if they knew the prostitutes were taking a break and were now unavailable. There was a small bandstand. Appropriately "Smoke Gets in Your Eyes" was playing on the jukebox. *This place probably really gets going at night,* Anne thought. It was exactly the kind of place she had been looking for as she had looked in bars up and down Fillmore Street.

Anne kept waiting for the bartender to come over. He was talking to a cynical looking man and from what snatches of conversation she heard they were talking about the Korean War. Anne thought she was being snubbed and was about to leave when the bartender walked over and stood in front of her. He said nothing, just waited. Momentarily, Anne was speechless. She didn't know what to drink. In fact, other than a few glasses of wine she had not drunk alcohol before and definitely not alone in a bar. Finally, mostly because she couldn't think of anything else she asked hesitantly, "Could I please have a glass of orange juice." As if he were quite used to such a request the bartender reached under the counter, took out a bottle of orange juice, put some ice cubes in a glass, and poured it almost to the brim. "Two dollars," he said. Anne reached into her purse.

"Lean forward please. There is something I want to tell you," she said.

"Okay miss, but we don't share too many secrets here."

Anne whispered in his ear, "I want to buy a gun; and I don't want any men bothering me." She then put a twenty-dollar bill on the counter.

The bartender promptly gave her back eighteen dollars. He gave no indication he had even heard her. She had expected him to keep the twenty, maybe even ask for more. Anne gulped down half of her orange juice. Should she leave? she asked herself. Maybe she had been a bit forward. This was a bar and a jazz club in the evening. Maybe that was all there was to it. As she turned away from the bar and was about to get up, she almost bumped into a well-dressed white man in a business suit with padded shoulders. He was smoking a cigarette, dangling at a cocky angle from his lips. "Jack Daniels for the lady," he said to the bartender.

"Pay first," the bartender said.

"Sure," the man replied, and pulled out a twenty-dollar bill from his wallet.

The bartender walked over to the far end of the bar and said something to the cop who nodded but continued joking with the black prostitute. After a few minutes the cop got up and walked over to the man in the business suit who was waiting impatiently for his drink.

"May I see your identification please?"

Reluctantly the man took out his wallet and flipped it open to his driver's license.

"Take it out."

With a pained look on his face the man took out his driver's license.

"Satisfied? Look. I'm a computer programmer from Palo Alto. If there's any trouble I can contact my attorney."

"Save it. I'm citing you for smoking."

"Damn, I'm going to call my attorney."

"Don't get smart. Here's your citation and your license. Now leave."

The man started to pull out a cell phone, but the cop knocked it out of his hand, then kicked it under the table.

"Now leave."

The man walked out of the door with stooped shoulders which were quite obvious even beneath his shoulder pads.

The cop walked back to the stool next to the black prostitute and everyone continued what they were doing as if nothing had happened. Anne sipped the rest of her orange juice while considering if she had come to the right place. One thing was for sure. The bartender had kept his word. No man had bothered her.

Although Anne had not been hassled, she had sat there for some time and no one had approached her about selling a gun. In a place like this it was obvious that it was best not to ask why. If the matter was dropped it was dropped. As she started to get up, she felt a light tap on her shoulder. Another guy trying to put the make on her she thought. Well, the bartender would soon fix him. Anne turned around and found herself looking at the largest black man she had ever seen. His shoulders seemed as broad as she was tall, he had no neck, and his chest, belly, and legs were massive. His build was much like a sumo wrestler's. Fat but solid.

"You want to buy something?"

"Yes," she replied in a frightened voice.

"I'll meet you outside," he said with a warm smile.

He walked outside, and after a few minutes Anne followed him. She blinked her eyes several times, trying to get used to the sunlight. Even after the dim light in the bar, she had no trouble recognizing him.

"They call me Big Man," he said, chuckling as if he were amused at this own nickname. "This is Frank, and my other friend is Kirk." Both men were athletic-looking black men dressed in sports coats and slacks. They did not look particularly criminal nor did he for that matter.

"First your I.D."

Anne fished in her purse, pulled out her wallet, and showed him her California ID.

"Put it away," he said, after barely glancing at it.

"Now, before we begin there is one question I want to ask you, and answer me truthfully."

What was it? Was this an undercover sting operation? Anne wondered.

"If you want to buy a weapon, why don't you go to Chinatown?"

Anne breathed a sigh of relief. "Because I don't trust the Chinese mob men," she answered truthfully.

"Hear that?" Big Man said turning to his friends. "Hear that. Now listen to what she said. She trusts a black man more than she does a Chinese. You won't hear that on television or read it in the papers. But it's the Lord's truth." He started to laugh until his sides shook. His friends followed suit, only finishing when each slapped the palm of the other's hand.

"Look, little Chinese sister. I like you. Now maybe we better talk business. Here slip inside."

Big man opened the passenger side door of a white van with no windows. He motioned for Anne to get in. He now walked around the van and sat on the driver's seat. Frank and Kirk opened the side sliding door and sat behind them.

"Before I sell you anything lady, I want you to listen to me," Big Man announced. "You want to buy a gun from me, not a gun shop. I take it you want to kill somebody. Now, I'm going to tell you a few hard facts. One thing... ever fired a rifle or a pistol before?"

"No," Anne replied.

"I'm going to sell you a .357 Magnum with a silencer. Here's what I want you to do. The recoil will shock you. So you may not get an accurate second shot. I want you to brace the Magnum against something. Hold it with both hands, and slowly squeeze the trigger. Whoever it is you're trying to knock off, ambush him, surprise him. Practice what you're going to do. Run through it a few times. Go for something big: the chest, the stomach. Drop him on the first shot, then take a couple more. Make sure he's dead. And no bullshit last minute conversations like in the movies. Lastly, drop the gun off the Golden Gate Bridge. Or get rid of it so no one will ever find it.

"I'm telling you this for my own good. If they catch you, then maybe they catch me; and I won't like that nor will my friends. Now, got $700?"

Anne opened her purse. She had brought ten one-hundred-dollar bills. With trembling hands, she took out all ten of them.

"Seven hundred. That's it," Big Man said emphatically while taking seven one-hundred-dollar bills.

"Here's the gun. It is loaded and ready."

One of the men sitting behind her handed her a Real Foods cloth shopping bag. She looked into the bag. All she could see were several packages of ramen noodles. But as she lifted the bag by the handles it felt quite heavy.

"Now goodbye and remember what I told you," Big Man said.

Anne got out of the van. She held tightly onto the shopping bag. She walked over to the 38 Geary bus stop and stood next to an elderly Chinese woman and a blonde teenage girl with a gold nose ring. They didn't know who she really was, Anne thought. They didn't know who she had really become.

42

Anne waited in the darkness. She had the kitchen window cracked open, and the curtain drawn down. The muzzle of the .357 Magnum was propped up by two cans of sardines on the window sill against which the handle of the pistol also rested. That way the muzzle would not depress too far and would be braced, and the handle would be braced against the sill. The Magnum was pointed at the chest of anyone who stood in front of the front door. Ten o'clock had come and gone and there was still no sign of the chauffeur. Anne kept trying to go over in her mind what she was going to do, but she kept thinking of Yoshi, of having his sweet cock in her mouth while she teased his testicles with her fingernails. Why couldn't she be more focused at a time like this? Or at least think of Geary. Silently she said Yoshi's name.

She thought she heard something, like quiet footsteps approaching, then suddenly she saw the chauffeur's shadowy form. He knocked on the door several times, sharply, quickly as if he already owned the building. Anne had practiced this several times. She left the Magnum where it was, walked over, unlocked the door, making sure she made plenty of noise, but she left the sliding bolt secured. "Come in," she said. Anne quickly stepped back to the window. There was the chauffeur turning the door handle, and vainly trying to push the door open. She now had the Magnum in position. She aimed. She squeezed the trigger. Bang. She saw blood spurt out of the chauffeur's chest. She grabbed the Magnum, unbolted and opened the front door. The chauffeur was sprawled out at her feet. She pulled the trigger. One shot through the head, then another one. Anne closed the door, locked, and bolted it.

"I did it right," Anne said to herself. "I did it right." She put the Magnum down on the kitchen table. *Big Man would be proud,* she thought. And then another thought. One that she wished she had not thought. The body was in front of her door, and she did not know how to get rid of it.

She thought of phoning Yuan. No. How crazy. Blossom Wong? Maybe she could help? Anne dialed her number, misdialed it, then dialed it again.

"Blossom Wong. This is Anne."

"What is it dear? You are not due here until Friday."

"No, no. I need your help. Let me explain."

Anne quickly went over what had just happened.

"Anne dear, do as I say. Throw a blanket over the body so people will think it's a street person asleep, then come immediately over here and bring the gun with you. Be quick."

Anne was going to say something when Blossom Wong hung up. What Blossom Wong had said was very obvious now that Anne thought about it. She rushed into the bedroom, pulled a blanket off the bed, opened the front door and threw the blanket on the body. She then went back in and put the Magnum in the Real Foods shopping bag, closed the door and ran down the alleyway. Her mind raced as she reached Stockton Street, but something told her she must slow down. She should not be seen as a fugitive.

There were not many people on Stockton Street, but Anne felt that every eye was on her and everyone knew exactly what had happened.

43

Every person Anne passed seemed like a ghost chasing her in the night. She wanted to run. She wanted to flee; but kept to a brisk pace until little by little she reached Quincy Alley.

The ritual with the bouncer went more quickly than usual, and when the door swung open, she felt at home. She felt safe. The bouncer said not one word but merely pointed to Blossom Wong's room. On the first knock Anne heard Blossom Wong say, "Come in please."

As Anne entered, she saw Blossom Wong standing impatiently in the middle of the room slowly fanning herself. "Please close the door dear," she said in a firm tone of voice. Anne closed the door, then turned around to face Blossom Wong, wishing it would all go away. "It's been taken care of completely dear. Blood and all," Blossom Wong said with an angry edge in her voice.

Anne could hardly believe her ears. Taken care of so quickly? Because of the short time involved, she suspected someone in the warehouse across the street had done it. Blossom Wong did not offer any further explanation, however, nor did Anne ask for one.

"Now dear, please hand me your gun."

Anne handed her the Real Foods shopping bag. Blossom Wong put it behind her inlaid jade dressing screen. Everything was such a relief that Anne's body felt limp, and she started to sit down in the chair behind her.

"I didn't tell you to be seated," Blossom Wong said sharply. "San San you have caused me much trouble. I have taken care of it in my own way, but you must never speak of this. Do you understand," she said, snapping her fan shut and hitting it against the heel of her hand.

"Yes," Anne replied.

"Good, in a few minutes I want you to put on a Qípáo and go out and sit in the parlor. I want as many people as possible to see you. If a customer asks for you, I will say that you are sick. It's unlikely, but you may need an alibi."

That certainly made sense, Anne thought as she now turned to go.

"I did not give you permission to leave," Blossom Wong barked.

This was too much for Anne. True, she had just committed murder, and Blossom Wong was covering for her, but Blossom Wong had always been warm, motherly, never like this... like a mean tyrant. Anne started to cry. She tried to control herself, but she kept sobbing almost like a little girl. Blossom Wong put her hand on Anne's shoulder.

"I'm sorry dear. Please sit down. It's all been too traumatic, hasn't it. This may be a place of pleasure, but it is also a business. It gets the best of me sometimes, like tonight. Here..."

Blossom Wong handed Anne a handkerchief. Anne wiped her tears.

"Keep it dear," Blossom Wong said sympathetically. "There's something I must add. I have done you a big favor. Now you must return it."

"I have some money." Anne replied.

"No. Money must not change hands and besides it may be more than you have on hand."

"Perhaps something else?"

"Yes. Something else. I have thought this over. You work here five, maybe seven times a month and that is the way I like it. I want my girls to be scarce not common. I want you," and then Blossom Wong paused for a moment, "to work here for the next three years."

Anne started to speak, but Blossom Wong cut her off.

"The customers like you, the girls like you, and you seem to enjoy your work," Blossom Wong said with a smile. "So this will not be a hardship will it?"

Anne started to laugh. No, it would definitely not be a hardship.

"I will do it," Anne replied, almost too eagerly.

"Good. Now put on a Qípáo and go out to the parlor."

44

Anne sat in the chair inlaid with mother of pearl and with the carved dragon heads at the ends of the armrests. She looked at the silk tapestry of a mountain with a man crossing a bridge in the rain. Why had Blossom Wong decided on three years? Did she have to pay off somebody, as Anne suspected? Perhaps the gang that was there that night across the street in Stark Alley? Who knew? It was best not to ask questions and to let this matter rest.

The bouncer ushered in a tall Chinese man with a shirt so white it almost hurt Anne's eyes. It contrasted wonderfully with his navy-blue suit. Anne had seen him here once or twice before, though until now she had never paid much attention to him. He stood in the middle of the room seemingly ill at ease. Finally, hesitantly, he walked up to Anne and said, "Excuse me. I am Hsing Chaun from Shanghai. Perhaps we can talk."

Anne almost laughed at his heavy accent when he spoke Cantonese. She was about to tell him that she regretted being ill. Blossom Wong, who was usually in her room but tonight had been sitting in her high-backed rattan chair across from her, walked quietly up behind him.

"Ah Mr. Chaun. How nice to see a man from Shanghai. Unfortunately, San San is not feeling well. Perhaps her friend Yan Yun."

"I'm sorry," Mr. Chaun said to Anne.

"I'll be better soon," Anne blurted out. Blossom Wong gave her a disapproving glance as if she wished Anne had kept her mouth shut.

"Yes, in a week or so, Mr. Chaun," Blossom Wong replied. "But not tonight." She then steered Mr. Chaun over to Yan Yun who stood up and bowed slightly when she was introduced.

She apparently said something funny, for Mr. Chaun laughed. Yan Yun turned to Anne and gave her a wink just before escorting him to a room.

Anne's hands clutched the dragon's heads on the armrests. She thought about the time she had been the go-down girl and of the time when she and Yan Yun had cured the man's bad hearing by rubbing their pussies against his ears. Or of the time when they had both licked a man's penis and fought playfully over who would have his semen spill into her mouth. Yes, she liked it here. Mr. Chaun would return or if not him another man she liked. Maybe she would even become a rich man's mistress. She would keep the laundry. It would be a simple living after taxes and overhead. Besides, she enjoyed the customers especially Mrs. Teng.

But working for three years several times a month at Blossom Wong's was certainly no punishment. She would enjoy every minute of it. It would be sexy, and it would be fun.

About the Author

Erich von Neff is a San Francisco longshoreman. He received his master's degree in philosophy from San Francisco State University and was a graduate research student at the University of Dundee Scotland.

Erich von Neff is well known on the French avant-garde and mainstream literary scenes. He is a member of the Poètes Français, La Sociétés des Poètes et Artistes de France, Vice Chancelier de la Federation Poetique de Saint Venance Fortunat, and Membre d'honneur du Caveau Stephanois. He has had the following publications in France (en français): Poems: 1252 Short Stories: 264 Small press books: 8 Prix (Prizes): 26.

Erich von Neff's novel "Prostitutées au bord de La Route" (Prostitutes by the Side of the Road) was published by "Cashiers de Nuit" (1999) with a grant from Centre Region des Lettres de Basse-Normandie.

Erich von Neff's book of poems "Les Putains Cocainomanes" (The Cocaine Whores) was published by Cahiers du Nuit, 1998. "Les Putains Cocainomanes " was discussed on 96.2 FM, Paris, 1998 by Marie-Andre Balbastre, Poem # 45 was read.

Several poems from "Les Putains Cocainomanes" were read at the Cafe Montmartre in Paris, 2010. Several poems from "Les Yeux qui faiblissent ont faim de la vigilance éternelle de la verité" were read at the Cafe Au Soleil de la Butte in Paris, 2014. Poems from "Un Cube chrome a l'interieur d'une coquille d'oeuf cassee" were read at the Cafe Au Soleil de la Butte in Paris 2014. A Trophée Victor Hugo was awarded to Erich von Neff's novel "Une Lancia rouge Devale Lombard Street a tombeau ouvert," (The Red Lancia Roars Down Lombard Street), 1998.

Several poems from "Le Puttane della cocaina" (The Cocaine Whores) were read by Giulia Lombardo at the Caffe Litterario in Rome, at the Caffe Palatennistavolo, Teni Italy & Caffe degli artisti in Milan, Bookbar in Rome, Bibliocafe in Rome, and in five other Italian cafes in Italy, 2014. Several poems from "Le Puttane della cocaina" were read by Giulia Lombardo at the Caffe Palatennistavolo,

Terni Italy in February. Six readings in May 2015, three readings in June 2015, two readings in July, four readings in August, four readings in September, three readings in October, five readings in December 2015. Two readings of "Le Puttane dela cocaina" were read by Giulia Lombardo at the Caffe Palatennistavolo, Terni Italy, January 2016. Two readings of "Le Puttane della cocaina" were read by Giulia Lombardo at the Caffe Palatennistavolo, February 2016.

The poetry book "Un Cube Chrome a L'Interieur d'une Coquille d'Oeut Cassee" was published by Henri Tramoy editeur of Soleils et Cendre, France, 2016. In 2018, 30 short stories and three poems were published in Russian magazines. In 2019 the book of poems Le Cabaret de la Souris Rugissante (The Cabaret of the Roaring Mouse) was published by Atlier de l'agnew, editor Francoise Favretto. "Le Cabaret de la Souis Rugissante" was awarded a Trophée Edgar Allen Poe by Simone Gabriel editor of Cepal magazine. "Le Cabaret de la Souris Rugissante" was read by translator Jean Hautepierre at L'Autre Livre bookstore in Paris on September 5th. It was also read by Jean Hautepierre at the Cafe de la Marie in Paris on October 15th. It was read by the French actor Sebastien Bidault at the Bar-Restaurant du Palais in Paris on December 18th. There were four good reviews.

Glossary

Abacus: A frame holding parallel rods strung with movable beads that is used for manual computation. *Webster's Riverside II Dictionary*, 1996, page 1

Cìxiù shàngyì: Embroidered silk blouse

Húgín: The Chinese violin. It is made of bamboo, has two strings and is played with a bow. It is very high pitched. *Secrets of the Chinese Drama*, Cecilia Zung. 1964, page 31

Origami: The Japanese art of folding paper into decorative shapes. *Webster's II Riverside Dictionary*, 1996, page 484

Pei: Chinese opera robe. Somewhat similar to a Japanese Kimono. *Secrets of the Chinese Drama*, Cecila Zung, 1964, page 21

Qì: Energy, vital force.

Qípáo: A formal Chinese woman's silk dress with a slit up the sides and a Mandarin collar.

Shang Dynasty: 1523 B.C. to 1027 B.C.

Xiäo: A flute held parallel to the lips, the instrument being to the right. *Secrets of the Chinese Drama*, 1964, page 32

Yuèqín: A moon-shaped guitar with four strings used to assist the Húgín. *Secrets of the Chinese Drama* Cecilia Zung, 1964, page 32

Yuan Dynasty: 1279 A.D. to 1368 A.D.

This glossary was prepared with the help of Professor Chris Wen-Chao Li of San Francisco State University.

Secondary Glossary

Anna May Wong: 1905-1961. A Chinese American film actress popular during the 1930's.

Ainu: A member of the indigenous people inhabiting the northernmost islands of Japan. They are very hairy.

Auntie: An honorific bestowed on older Chinese women.

Bilibid Concentration Camp: A Japanese prisoner of war concentration camp in the Philippines during World War II.

Boxer Rebellion: 1898-1900.

Buddy Bolen: New Orleans coronet player, 1877-1934.

Bunk Johnson: 1889-1949. New Orleans trumpet player and jazz band leader often with **George Lewis**, 1900-1968, on clarinet.

Chinatown Post Office: 1867 Stockton Street, San Francisco.

Chow Fun: A dish made with noodles, meat, vegetables and sauce.

Eternity Jewelery: 751 Grant Avenue in San Francisco's Chinatown.

Fiesole: An old Etruscan town above Florence.

Hotel Kabuki: 1625 Post Street, San Francisco.

Ikebana: Japanese flower arrangement.

Joseph Yan Art Gallery: 125 Clement Street, San Francisco.

Mai's Vietnamese Restaurant: 316 Clement Street, San Francisco.

Mary Thē: Skin care shop at 153 Maiden Lane, San Francisco.

New Chinatown or Golden Gate Post Office: 3245 Geary Boulevard, San Francisco.

Pacific Autocare: 901 Pacific Avenue.

Palanquin: A covered litter for one person that is carried on poles on the shoulders of men.

Ramen: Long, thin Chinese noodles.

Sun Sang Market: 1205 Stockton Street.

Tan: A female impersonator in the Chinese opera.

Young Tigers: The Japanese use this term rather than "young Turks".